A Girlfriend for Christmas

BARBARA WINKES

For D.

Chapter One

CINDY

My workday was about to wind down when Alison Carter came out of Mrs. Regan's office looking frustrated and lost. I was on my feet before I knew it.

"Good evening, Ms. Carter. Can I help you with anything?" Polite, and a bit too eager.

"I need a girlfriend," she answered.

I had a hard time keeping my composure and resisting the urge to pinch myself. It was late. Perhaps I misunderstood. I might be hallucinating, or daydreaming. All of it was more likely than Alison Carter saying these words to me.

If it happened for real, we'd be talking about a true Christmas miracle, and I didn't believe in those. Did I? Seconds ticked by, and I realized I was still staring at her.

"I'm so sorry," Alison said, her cheeks flushed with embarrassment. "I don't know why I said that. Have a good evening. Merry Christmas."

She walked out of the office in brisk steps, and I stood frozen, until the sound of the door jolted me into motion. There had to be a reason why she'd answered my words with something other than a meaningless nicety. I had to find out what she meant, if only to make sure I hadn't made the whole scene up.

I caught up with her in the stairwell.

"Ms. Carter, please, wait. I'm not sure I understood..."

"That's all right. I said forget about it."

I winced at her impatient tone. Alison was my boss's niece. She owned a business as well, creating social media and overall branding solutions for her clients, which included my employer. We had exchanged few words. She came in every once in a while to talk to Mrs. Regan, and I provided coffee, tea or snacks, depending on the occasion. Once, Mrs. Regan had sent me for a bottle of champagne. Today didn't appear to be an occasion for celebration, even though Christmas was less than a couple of weeks away.

"If I can do anything..." I'm not sure what I thought I could achieve other than get her annoyed with me and have her complain to Mrs. Regan, but I was on a mission. This might be an opportunity that would never come back again. To my relief, she didn't run away but leaned against the wall and sighed.

"It's complicated. You don't want to get involved in this."

"Why did you say that to me?"

She looked at me long enough to make me fidget, a wry smile tugging at the corners of her mouth. I was grateful for the dim lighting out here. My cheeks were burning.

"Aunt Bella always calls you a miracle worker."

"She does?"

"I could use a miracle," she admitted. "But that's not your problem."

"Maybe, but you're Mrs. Regan's family, and she's the best boss I've ever had. If I can help with anything, I'll do whatever I can."

"That sounds nice."

I thought I got her, but she shook her head. "You have to get back to work."

"Yes, eventually, but I was done for the day. I just have to get my coat and purse."

That was...almost true. I waited, giving her one more chance to tell me that I was crazy, and should leave her alone. Instead, she said, "All right. I'll wait for you in my car. Let's go eat something, and I'll tell you the whole sad story."

"I'm sure it's not that bad. I'll be right there."

I didn't waste any time wondering how I had even managed to speak in full sentences to her about something that didn't have to do with coffee or pastries. Back at my desk, I turned off my computer and picked up my coat and purse as quickly as humanly possible. Through the glass door, I saw that Mrs. Regan was on the phone, so I waved to her. I'd explain my rushed exit tomorrow. After all the overtime I'd put in lately, I didn't think she was going to fire me.

I headed to the elevators, all of them slow. Cursing or hitting the button a few extra times, surprise, didn't make a difference. It took about four minutes for me to get to the parking garage, and Alison's Lexus that I had admired a few times before. It felt more like an hour, but to my relief, she didn't appear impatient. In fact, I caught her leaning back in the driver's seat with her eyes closed. Suppressing a sigh, I carefully opened the door to sit next to her, and she straightened.

"There you are. I have to admit, you don't give up easily. Let's go."

I was in the car with Alison Carter, about to go out for dinner. My life couldn't be more perfect.

3

The drive to the restaurant was a short one. Alison didn't talk. I didn't mind, too preoccupied with taking in the present moment. My first doubts started to creep in when, after she'd parked in front of the place, Alison handed the keys to the valet. That kind of restaurant.

I was fairly sure I'd be able to cover my bill with the credit card, but from there it would be PB & jelly sandwiches for the rest of the month. It wasn't that Mrs. Regan didn't pay me enough, but rent was a big chunk of my monthly expenses.

Who cared?

I was lucky to have come straight from work. I was still woefully underdressed in my slacks and blouse, but it could have been worse. Last Friday, we had an ugly Christmas sweater day.

Alison knew her way around, though, a regular from the looks of it. I wasn't surprised. The hostess led us to a table in the back, next to the window. The place was all decked out for Christmas, though decorations were somewhat restrained and tastefully arranged, in muted tones that fit the rest of the interior. A tall tree decorated in red and silver stood near an impressive fireplace.

Seconds after we'd sat down, a waitress brought the menus and asked for our drink of choice.

My sudden discomfort must have shown. Alison ordered a bottle of white wine for both of us.

"If you agree? This one is very versatile."

"Yes. Sure."

Once we'd ordered, she leaned back into her seat, studying me.

"I'm aware I owe you an apology for springing this on you."

"Oh no, that's fine—"

"An explanation, then, okay? I swear I don't go around making propositions like this. Today was...challenging."

It had to be. This was the most she had spoken to me—ever. Sometimes I wasn't even sure she noticed me, and that was fine too, at the time. I couldn't go there. I couldn't process that Alison seemed to have acknowledged me beyond her aunt's helpful assistant, because that would make it complicated. Awkward. I liked to think I was in control of the situation. In my dreams.

"So how can I help you?"

"I put myself into a pretty bizarre situation. A situation where I need to convince my friends that I am in a relationship."

"Mrs. Regan too?"

"No, this has nothing to do with her. You'll probably think it's ridiculous."

"Try me."

She took a sip of her wine. Next, appetizers arrived, and that was the last reprieve either of us got.

"I like my job, okay? I like being in charge. I'm good at that."

Never in a million years would I have doubted that.

"I'm not sure I'm connecting the dots yet," I admitted. I was intrigued though. So, so much.

"I am going on a trip this coming weekend. A secluded luxury cabin in the snow, with all the bells and whistles you can imagine."

"Oh. Good for you." Much as I liked her, I was proud of myself for saying this without the slightest hint of sarcasm. People like her and Mrs. Regan lived in a different world. I wasn't jealous. Not much, anyway.

"These are good, well-meaning people, but for some reason, they don't understand this one thing about me. I don't want a relationship. With anyone."

We both picked up our glasses at the same time. Alison, because she might be embarrassed about revealing something so personal to someone she didn't know at all—me, because her words served as the equivalent of a cold shower. On the bright side, I was starting to understand her dilemma, or what she considered to be one.

"It's Christmas, and they're your friends, right? I'm sure they'll listen if you try to explain..."

Alison waved her hand in a dismissive gesture.

"Even if I wanted to...They already invited an amazing guy, self-made, incredibly successful, single and looking."

I wasn't sure if the wine or her presence made it harder to think, but I felt like I understood less, the more I learned. Or maybe I was starting to understand perfectly, and the picture didn't fit the one I wanted to have of her.

"You said you needed a girlfriend. Why?"

"I think that would make it easier on everyone."

Could she really be this naïve? What was I still doing here?

"Okay. So not only are you planning to lie to your friends, you want to make the lie special?"

For some reason I didn't want to look at too closely, I was disappointed to find out she was just another straight woman who thought it was okay to play gay to get out of an uncomfortable situation. How did that happen? If I was honest, I didn't know her either. I did know that she was my boss's niece, so I should stay polite, but I couldn't help myself.

To my surprise, she wasn't mad at me.

"No, you didn't understand me. If I wanted to date, and if I had time to find someone before that weekend, that person would be a woman. But since neither one is an option right now, I had this weird idea that I could convince someone to pretend for a few days to get them off my back permanently. If they think I'm in a relationship, they'll stop trying to set me up with guys."

"You haven't come out to them," I concluded. "Wow, this *is* complicated."

"No kidding," she said and filled my glass again. "Now that I've bared my soul to you, what do you say? You think you could handle a few days as my surprise guest?"

This felt like a genie was dangling three wishes in front of me, right before I'd make a life-changing decision that would get me in so much trouble.

"I don't know," I said honestly. "You want it to be convincing?"

I had lost my mind, there was no other explanation.

"That's the plan."

"Why me?"

"I was thinking about how little time I had to convince someone, and you were there...I'm sorry, that didn't come out right," Alison corrected herself right away, though neither of us could hide from the truth of her statement. She wasn't looking for a date, let alone a relationship. She needed someone to play a part in a charade, and I was, well, convenient. This was me. Convenient was my middle name, just ask Mrs. Regan.

I might get to kiss her.

"Where are we going?"

Alison looked relieved. "You don't have to worry about a thing. You'd be doing me the biggest favor anyone has ever done me. Give me a couple of days and I'll arrange plane tickets, and everything else."

It wasn't until then that I realized how desperate she was to make this happen. I had enough doubts already. Would she think I was taking advantage of her?

"You don't have to do that."

"I think I have to. I'm not sure you'd be able to afford it otherwise."

All right then. Different worlds. I had to admit that between the two of us, there were no false pretenses. She had presented the situation to me in the most honest way, and besides, I guessed I had already said yes.

"Okay. I think we can hash out the details on the way there."

"Thank you so much, Sydney."

"You're welcome...but it's Cindy."

"Cindy. I'm so sorry."

"That's okay. I can call you Alison? I mean...I think I should start, if we don't want to slip up."

Alison looked as if I'd just taken the greatest weight off her shoulders. I still wasn't sure if this was a good idea in the long run, but there was no way I could back out. I didn't want to. I had the chance to do Alison Carter a favor. No person in their right mind would say no to what she offered.

"Sure."

"So...Is there anything I should know? The people I'll meet there? We should be thinking about a story, how we met, etc."

She had called me Sydney, there was that...I was determined to make sure she'd remember my name, and the favor I'd done her.

"That's okay," she said. "Like you said, we'll talk about it on the way. Thank you."

ALISON

Now that was embarrassing. As I let myself into my condo later that night, I cringed hard at the memory of letting those words slip out. In front of the miracle worker, no less. It looked like Cindy, Aunt Bella's favorite assistant, was going to provide one for me, even after I got her name wrong.

In return she deserved nothing less than being treated to a luxurious outing. Some things can't be taken back though. She'd forever know my sad secret. I'd get a reprieve, not much else. It had to do for now. I wasn't planning on creating drama when we'd only be together for a few days.

Fortunately, I was ahead of the game, thanks to my aunt. She had business connections with Jim and Nancy who had invited my designated blind date. They hadn't called him that, and neither had Aunt Bella, but I wasn't fooled.

I slipped out of my coat and dropped my purse near the door, heading straight for the bathroom where I ran a hot bath. Before undressing, I made a beeline for the kitchen, taking out a glass and an open bottle of wine out of the fridge. Comforts of a happy single person. I was. Even at Christmas. The omnipresent music and decorations didn't bother me. I'd probably work and enjoy the quiet time at the office, while everyone else was stressed out trying to live up to impossible expectations of the perfect holidays.

I wasn't sad, or lonely, except Cindy likely thought I was.

Did that bother me? I barely knew anything about her, why would I care what she thought? I filed that question away for another time, got into the bath and leaned back into the bubbles with a content sigh.

It could be worse, right? I had to admit I enjoyed the evening. Despite the rocky start, Cindy was easy to talk to. Maybe it was her personality, or her job had given her the skills to deal with people like me, people like my friends...She'd be fine. The friendly nagging would finally stop, and we could all go back to our lives.

No need to make any changes.

If this was a defeat, not coming out with the whole truth, so to speak, so be it. It was the best possible solution, other than spending even more energy on pointless discussions on why I didn't want to go on dates. I knew there was nothing wrong with me. I had become tired of explaining it to other people, no matter how well-meaning.

It was much easier and effective to spend some money on Cindy who was so eager to help—easy on the eyes, too.

I felt a little sorry for the guy they'd invited for me...but not that much.

"Merry Christmas to me," I said out loud. I was still embarrassed, but the trip didn't look all that daunting to me any longer.

Chapter Two

CINDY

I was so deeply in denial I wouldn't have been able to find my way out to save my life. Could anyone blame me? I remembered the day and the hour Mrs. Regan first introduced me to Alison. Well, that was a big word. She and Alison had a working breakfast together, and Mrs. Regan had asked me to arrange something. When I brought them a coffee refill, she said, "Cindy did a great job putting this together."

Alison had looked up, smiled, and forgotten about me, or, at least, my name.

Today, everything had changed. She needed me. Maybe what she said meant she had dated women, or would at some point be open to, but that's not where we were. We'd pretend so her friends wouldn't find out how fed up she was with their meddling. Was this a good thing? A bad thing?

For sure, it was an "Under no circumstances can I tell her no" thing. I'd been quietly harboring my crush on her for over a year now. I had no illusions. After the long weekend, Alison planned to break up with her pretend girlfriend, but part of me was stubbornly optimistic: A lot could happen in four days.

Yeah, right.

As I sat in my bathtub later, pondering the unexpected events of the day, I thought I knew exactly what I was in for.

The once-in-a-lifetime, temporary opportunity with a woman who was far out of my league. I was excited, and scared, because I also knew that the most likely outcome of it was heartbreak. At this moment, I didn't care.

⋅♥⋅♥⋅♥⋅♥⋅♥⋅

Reality caught up with me swiftly the next day, when I had to go back to work and explain to Mrs. Regan why I needed some time off, let alone at this time of the year. I knocked on the door of her office, her favorite latte and bagel in hand.

"Good morning, Mrs. Regan."

She barely looked up from her papers. "Morning, Cindy. Thanks."

Perhaps I shouldn't bother her with this first thing...but I needed to prepare, examine my closet and maybe do some shopping. Alison had promised that everything would be paid for, but I wasn't sure my wardrobe was believable for someone pretending to be her girlfriend.

The thought never failed to fill me with excitement and glee. I could feel the silly smile form on my face as I started to fidget. Her girlfriend.

"Is there anything else?"

"Um...Yes." It was now or never. "I need to ask you something. I...I was wondering if I could take Friday and Monday off. And..." I had never asked for anything like this before. I was starting to feel a little sick, thinking I might have overestimated myself. "If I could leave a little earlier on Thursday?" For a few seconds, she was silent, and I was sure that would be it. She'd think I lost my mind and fire me.

"Yeah, sure." She put a sheet into a folder and picked up another one.

I still stood in the same place, frozen in disbelief. It couldn't be that easy?

Mrs. Regan looked up at me, a hint of impatience to her expression.

"I'm sorry, Cindy, but I am really busy. You can talk to Sonia about what she needs to handle in your absence."

"Okay...Thank you."

"Alison told me she'd like to borrow you for a project. It's fine."

That did nothing to get me to move, on the contrary.

"She...did?"

"Yes, she said you talked the other day. I need to get back to work now, and I think you do, too."

"Yes, Mrs. Regan. Of course."

The reality of what I had agreed to came crashing down on me. I was going to be Alison's fake girlfriend for the weekend trip, and I had to be believable if I still wanted her to talk to me after the "job."

Fortunately, the day was fairly busy. I couldn't obsess about the upcoming getaway even if I'd wanted to. Instead, after work, I called my friend Irin to schedule an impromptu shopping afternoon, and after that, a night out.

Truth be told, I had no idea what would be appropriate. Alison was a successful businesswoman, and I assumed that her friends would be the same. Money was not a problem.

She had paid for my dinner, and she'd cover all my expenses involved in getting to the destination. I owed her, but I would have liked a little more guidance. I had sent a text message to the number Alison had given me but didn't hear from her...I would have to make things up as I went along. I had the unsettling feeling that this wouldn't go for clothes only.

Irin met me at the mall.

"That's a nice surprise, you getting off work before the stores close," she said as a greeting, hugging me.

"You don't know the half of it," I mumbled.

"Is everything okay?"

"Oh yes, everything is great. I need a few items to wear that look a lot more expensive than they are."

"You've asked the right person." Irin laughed. "I make sure that everything I wear looks more expensive than it is. Fake it until you make it, right?"

That made me wince, even though she had no idea about my plans.

"Something like that. I need a couple of casual outfits, a dress I guess, oh, and new PJs." For some reason that made me blush.

Irin studied me curiously. "You're going somewhere? Wait! You met someone? It must have been at work, right? Given that it's where you spend all your waking hours."

"Come on, it's not that bad," I protested.

"It is that bad. Who is she?"

"It's not what you think. I'm doing someone a favor."

"Who?"

"Alison Carter." I tried to make my face behave. I had to sell the news like it was no big deal, but I couldn't stop smiling. This was my once-in-a-lifetime opportunity. A winter vacation with Alison. Forget about worries, this was already the best Christmas present ever.

Irin's eyes widened. Either she was speechless, or she was trying to figure out something to say without hurting my feelings in case I made it up.

"The Alison Carter you've been crushing on forever? What's the favor?"

"Long story. And it hasn't been forever. I'll tell you all about it, but first I need to update my wardrobe."

"I'm curious. Let's get started. I have a few ideas."

At the end of a rather exhausting shopping spree, I had a couple of bags filled with pieces that I thought would pair reasonably well with my existing wardrobe and not tip anyone off. Did I need the little black dress? Who could blame me for the fantasy?

After taking advantage of Irin's expertise, I owed her a little more information. I paid my dues when we sat down for appetizers and drinks.

"But didn't you say she was straight?"

"I was wrong. Maybe she's bi, I don't know. In any case, she's tired of her friends setting her up, and she asked me to help her out." Saying it out loud, I had to admit it sounded odd.

"And she can't tell them to knock it off? Why go to all the trouble of finding a fake girlfriend?"

How would I know? I got lucky, that's all there was to the story—on my side of it, anyway.

"I don't know, but I guess I'm going to find out when I meet them."

"Be careful. She might be taking advantage of you."

That would be wrong, how exactly? I was starting to get impatient with Irin. Before last night, Alison had barely spoken to me, and she didn't have much of a reason. This was different. Much better.

"What do you mean? I know she's not interested in a relationship."

"Does she know how you feel about her?"

"Are you crazy? Of course not."

"I don't know. It seems like you're in over your head."

I didn't like hearing that at all, especially after I'd spent almost a thousand dollars on clothing.

"It's only for a few days, then I'll go spend Christmas with my folks. It will be fun, I'm sure. She doesn't owe me anything."

"Well, if you're sure, that's all that matters."

"It'll be fine. I know what I'm in for."

Irin was nice enough not to question what might have been a blatant lie.

ALISON

C indy had sent a text message with a few questions regarding "our story." I set the phone aside and sipped my coffee, wondering why I was nervous all of a sudden. There was no story. She knew that. We would go over a few points on the way, make sure we didn't slip up. The fewer details we came up with, the fewer chances someone might catch us in a lie.

I counted on everyone being so stunned they wouldn't have any questions. Or they'd have too many.

Was I about to make a big mistake?

I might be a bit hypocritical about it all—I could have said no to the trip, stay away, but the truth was, I loved those people, and I was looking forward to spending time with them. Nancy was hilarious. Jim made the best Manhattans on the planet. Lauren and Kelli were adorable, even though I couldn't imagine that kind of lifestyle, marriage and parenthood, for myself. If only they'd all stopped doing this thing...

I was busy wrapping up last-minute paperwork, but when my phone rang, I picked it up anyway.

"We are leaving in a bit, but I had to call you. We're so excited!"

Did Kelli know something already? Aunt Bella wouldn't interfere...she couldn't know?

"That's great," I said cautiously.

"This is going to be amazing. I was going to tell everyone at the same time, but...We found a donor!"

"Wow, that's amazing news! Congratulations."

"Thank you. To be honest, we were a little worried you might not make it. I look forward to seeing you."

"What are you saying? I wouldn't miss this weekend for anything." Okay, that might be a bit of an exaggeration, but only because they were so oblivious when it came to this particular subject. I was happy for them, their milestones, their families. I wish they could see that different things mattered to me.

I wasn't sad.

It had taken me only a heartbeat to find a fake girlfriend. I had a good life, and serious skills.

"Good. Can't wait to see you."

"You too. And Jim's Manhattans."

"Yeah, though Lauren will want to take it easy, and I want to be supportive. We do have a surprise for you, though."

Yeah, I know what you're talking about, I thought, frowning. I didn't want to get into that.

Alice, my secretary, waved from the door, perfect timing.

"I have one for you, too," I said. "I'm sorry, I have to go. See you all soon."

Now that I had found my almost perfect solution, I hoped no one would put a wrench in my plans.

I realized I still hadn't texted Cindy back, so I sent a quick message to meet me at the airport. *Don't forget to pack warm winter clothes and a bathing suit.* I'd take care of the rest. The way I liked it. Then I got up to join Alice.

"Mr. Matthews is on line two," she said. "He asked if you'd go over the numbers with him one more time, then he'd be ready to sign."

I didn't even think I'd be able to file away that contract before the holidays.

"That's good news. I'll head over there, and we can take care of it now."

Miracle worker or good luck charm, Cindy's presence in my life was already making it better. With a smile, I picked up the phone.

"Mr. Matthews, it's good to hear from you."

The weekend would be even better. I had earned it.

Chapter Three

CINDY

Alison met me at the airport and took me to the lounge to have breakfast. I might have objected more to her paying for things if I hadn't invested this much in items like the cute, but too cold coat she didn't comment on at all. I might be freezing for nothing...but it was still early.

I enjoyed breakfast, though I was starting to have butterflies in my stomach for various reasons. This was getting real, pretending to be in a relationship with a woman I barely knew, who knew nothing about me.

"So...How are we going to do this?"

Alison seemed relaxed, her mind not troubled by the same subject that had occupied mine since the moment I said yes.

"I just need you to be there, that's all."

"Really, you think they're going to believe us? Shouldn't we, I don't know, come up with a good story? I should know a little more about you." I wanted to. I realized she might not return the sentiment.

"They're not going to ask too many details, believe me. It's a weekend of hanging out, too much of too rich food and booze. We can say we met at work. Anything else is none of their business."

That shut me up for a while, but it also made me wonder about her friends. Wouldn't they want to know more? Why not? If either of us slipped up, would they even care? If none of it was a big deal, why the pretense in the first place?

"Don't worry about it," she said. "You'll be fine."

That was debatable when I still had to get over the fact that I was here, with her. I knew she was reserved most of the time, private, but I'd heard her laugh out loud at something when she was in the office with Mrs. Regan. I understood enough to relate. I liked my job and my career too, even though I thought I might be more open to make time for the right person, if they came along.

Not that Alison fit the bill. She couldn't, because she didn't want anyone in her life, and I wasn't going to invite predictable heartbreak into mine, no matter what Irin said. I preferred to have a few close friends who knew me well, rather than many casual acquaintances.

Did anyone know Alison well? Did she let anybody?

None of my business, I reminded myself.

"I am thirty-six. I love a good red wine, I strongly dislike mushrooms. Someone's going to try and make me go skiing, no matter how many times I told them I'm not inclined. Your turn."

I had to do better than doing my deer-in-the-headlights routine whenever she looked at me like that—though it might help the charade. I wasn't sure if I could count any of those as revelations, but I went with it.

"I just turned thirty. I love pizza and ice cream. I'd love to go to Italy someday...I also enjoy everything about Christmas, the

decorations, spending time with friends and family, the food..."
Why did her words sound like normal conversation, and mine
like mindless rambling? I felt my cheeks heat once more. "Your
friends, are they all married? Do they have children?"

"Nancy and Jim do, but the getaway is adults only. Kelli and
Lauren want to have a baby next year, so expect a lot of talk
about that."

The story was getting more mysterious by the minute. Coming out, it seemed, wouldn't be a big deal. Why couldn't she
tell them she liked being single? What could they do about
it? Perhaps it was a good time to remind myself not to look a
gift horse in the mouth, not that I'd compare either of us to a
horse...even my thoughts were in complete disarray.

"Sure, that's not a problem. Could you tell me a bit more
about what got you interested in your work, how you started out? I mean, they might think we've talked about that." I
thought that the job would be a subject she'd be more comfortable with. I was mistaken.

"We don't need to go into depth on this, and besides, we
should go. It will be time for boarding soon."

All right, then. I didn't want to admit that I was getting a bit
impatient with her reluctance to do anything to make this work.
On the bright side, if Alison turned out to be not half as nice as
I had imagined her, it would make a lot of things easier on me.

A win-win situation, no doubt about it.

ALISON

Cindy was watching me, trying not to be obvious about it. Huddled behind my laptop, I couldn't decide whether I found it endearing or unnerving. This was probably not what she had expected, but I hadn't given this idea as much thought as she might believe.

I thought she looked adorable in that blue coat though I hadn't mentioned it. We didn't have to pretend yet, and I didn't want to make her uncomfortable. I was trying the best I could.

Yet, I could sense her fidget in the seat next to me. Did she want to talk? What would we talk about?

We met at work, started dating, she had agreed to join me on the trip and meet my friends. What else was there to talk about? Besides, taking this many days off meant I had to do some work. She surely understood that.

I cast a quick sideways glance in her direction. Cindy looked away, blushing, confirming all my suspicions. I entertained the idea of packing up the computer for a bit and calling her out on it, but I was saved by the flight attendant who came through with her cart serving pastries.

"Anything to drink?" she asked.

"A coffee, please," I told her. "Milk and sugar."

"No, thanks," Cindy mumbled.

What had I been thinking?

There was no turning back now. I went back to my file and sipped my coffee, but I kept stealing glances. She was cute. If I had a type, someone like her might be it. I didn't need a type though, just a good actress. She'd do a great job.

CINDY

The next time we talked after boarding the plane was at our destination airport. Fortunately, I had thought of bringing my e-reader, though the amount of lesbian romance on it didn't help. I couldn't stop wanting to figure out what the problem was, when Alison had no problem admitting she was attracted to women, and she was in fact friends with a lesbian couple. Why did she choose me? Because there was no danger she'd ever be attracted to someone like me? I was safe?

The relative privacy we had from each other in first class didn't help with my dark thoughts. It was probably a good thing I didn't have an opportunity to voice them. In for a lot more than a penny...and I didn't want to prove Irin right. I could handle this.

I could work miracles.

"Okay, this is what's going to happen next," Alison instructed me as we walked through the smaller airport. "The shuttle is going to pick us up, and when we arrive there, people will want to have a cocktail after settling in."

"Nancy, Jim, Lauren and Kelli."

"Yeah, and mystery man," Alison said grimly. "Just go with the flow. You'll know what I mean."

I supposed that would be all the information she was going to give me. To be honest, I was curious. I hadn't even begun to process all the unexpected events in the recent days, the expensive restaurant, the credit card bill that would come with the new outfits, still making me cringe, flying first class...and here we were, Alison and Cindy, fake girlfriends for the next four days.

I was in a world of trouble but looking forward to it.

The shuttle turned out to be a small luxury bus to bring us out of the city and up into the mountains to breathtaking sights. I barely noticed Alison grumbling because the wi-fi was spotty. Our journey brought us far up, until the city in the distance looked like a miniature village, mountains covered in snow looming on the other side.

"This is beautiful."

"Yeah. There's a reason why I wanted to come." I turned around, not having expected an answer from Alison. In fact, she would have to talk to me a bit more if...I was beginning to think that I was the only one worried that Nancy, Jim, Lauren, Kelli and mystery man might not buy our act.

"I don't blame you." We drove past other resorts, beautiful cabins, until the last stretch. I noticed that she was sitting up straighter.

"Don't worry. It will be okay," I said, putting my hand over hers, my heart beating fast as if I'd done something forbidden.

With a sigh, she said, "One way or another, we'll find out soon."

Chapter Four

CINDY

In my job I had met a few wealthy people. Alison's friends, who greeted me with friendly caution, were no exception. They were all gathered in the living area when we arrived, getting to their feet almost in choreography.

"Look who's here!" A tall blonde stepped forward and embraced Alison. "It's so great you could make it. And you brought...?"

"Cindy," I supplied and reached out a hand. She shook it in a firm grip, her smile welcoming but curious.

"Hi Cindy. I'm Lauren."

"I thought this weekend would be a great opportunity to introduce Cindy to all of you. Since you've been bothering me forever to bring someone."

So far, so good. Everyone was all smiles and polite phrases, though I didn't miss the looks that passed between the couples, and the group of friends in general. I wondered what reason they might have to judge us—or me. Did I pass muster? Didn't I?

"That's great," the brunette who had introduced herself as Nancy, commented. "Now that we're all here, how about a cocktail?"

"I'll get on it," Jim promised. "Meanwhile, you could show Alison and Cindy their room, and—"

"Alison Carter! Hi."

I had almost forgotten mystery man, and judging from Alison's expression, the same was true for her. She looked baffled for a second, then composed herself.

"Marc Frasier. What a surprise."

"A good one, I hope. I didn't know I was going to meet you here either. I've been told no business during the weekend, but given this opportunity, I wonder if we could make an exception."

Alison laughed. It sounded a bit strained in my ears.

"I'll be happy to make time."

"Great."

"You are incorrigible," Kelli chastised. "This is how you take a vacation?"

"Let's see the room now," Alison said. "I can't wait for that cocktail."

I couldn't decipher all the clues, but I sensed that my—our—situation had just gotten more complicated. We followed Nancy along the hallway to a door she unlocked, and into the suite. I stayed in the doorway, my jaw dropping, every reservation and doubt forgotten in favor of more shallow sentiments. No matter who your friends were, if they invited you to a place like this, you couldn't say no. You'd be crazy to say no. A spacious sitting area right in front of the huge window looked extremely inviting. I cast a sideways glance at the bed—king size. It wouldn't be awkward or uncomfortable for either one of us.

"I'll leave you two to it," Nancy said cheerfully. "Don't take too long. You'll love those Manhattans Jim makes."

"I remember them being pretty good." Alison was still staring at the bed as if this was the first time it occurred to her that we'd be sharing one. I decided to give her some space and headed for the bathroom, unable to hold back the comment.

"Oh my God."

"Are you okay in there?"

Forget about all my emotional hang-ups. If I could take a bath in this spectacular tub, with the view of the city far in the distance, I could be happy. It was so beautiful, it looked unreal, and it would be even better once it was dark. This was an amazing place to spend a few days and relax.

When I didn't answer, Alison joined me in the bathroom.

"This is so great. Thank you so much for this opportunity." Before I knew what I was doing, I hugged her, the pleasure of holding her in my arms overriding any rational thought...until she gently disengaged herself.

"Let's hurry up. They're waiting for us."

Sure. I was curious about Frasier, but I assumed I'd have another chance to ask that question. It seemed like she hadn't known this was the guy they had planned to set her up with. But if she could fool them for a weekend and make a business connection, it was a win-win situation, wasn't it?

ALISON

Dusk was falling outside when we joined the others in the living area, and Jim distributed his famous Manhattans. They did a great job melting away any residual worries. Cindy was in love with the room and our surroundings in general. No one questioned her presence. If it was a surprise for anyone, they didn't mention it. Everything was going according to plan—perfectly.

"If all goes well, I'm not going to be skiing next year," Lauren said, referring to her and Kelli's baby plans. "So, who's going to join me tomorrow?"

"Not me," Kelli said. "I plan to spend all day in front of that gorgeous fireplace. What about you, Cindy?"

"Oh...I don't know how," Cindy answered, giving me a quick questioning look. "I never tried."

I tried to convey without words that this was an okay answer. Kelli wasn't done with the subject yet.

"Alison could show you. She's pretty good, but I guess she told you that."

It wasn't exactly what I'd told her. I had some lessons when I was younger, and I could hold my own around decent skiers. I doubted she'd want me to teach her, but I smiled and nodded. I got the feeling that we'd both be doing that a lot for the next few days. So be it. This was fairly easy. Cindy made it easier than I had expected.

Cindy

So far so good. After drinks and introductions, we had a light dinner which consisted of various cheeses, breads, and fruit. Everyone was tired after the day of travel, so we didn't have to make up more of a story. Watching Alison comfortable in the presence of her friends, I could relax too. Until it was time to call it a night.

In the bathroom, I spent a little time enjoying the view. When I came out of it, Alison presented me with another, even more enjoyable view. I had trouble not staring. It was impossible not to notice how the satin nightgown hugged her curves, and why was she wearing something like this anyway, when it was freezing outside? Unless...I aborted the thought right away. It was more than warm enough in the room, and the heavy comforter would do the trick. She didn't need me for that.

"I know you're impressed with the surroundings, but would you come to bed?"

Was she mocking me?

"Sure."

"Sorry, I didn't mean anything by that," she said, sensing my uncertainty.

Well, it wasn't that difficult. I think I'd done okay, but we both knew I was far out of my league. Alison, her friends, this place.

"It's okay."

"You did great today."

"You mean that?" I asked as I slipped under the incredibly soft covers. This was heaven, on so many levels.

"I do. But we should go to sleep now. It's been a long day, and everyone will be up early." So they were as driven as she was, no surprise there. I remembered Kelli saying that she wanted to sit in front of the fireplace. The others would probably head out for various winter sports. That was none of my business.

"Okay. Good night."

"Good night, Cindy."

I stayed in my lane, so to speak, warm and comfy in a bedroom of a kind I'd only ever seen on a TV show, the woman I had a major crush on, next to me. Well, not exactly next to me, but not far away.

Merry Christmas to me.

.♥.♥.♥.♥.♥.

Alison did not stay in her lane. I woke up in the middle of the night realizing she had not only managed to pull most of the sheets over to her side, but also moved closer to me. A lot closer. I wasn't that cold, because she was fast asleep snuggled up against me, her head on my chest.

The first thoughts that sprang to mind were all catastrophic: What if she woke up? What if she woke up and thought I was responsible for this...position, or that I was trying to take advantage of her situation, of her? I should have known something like that would happen. Anything else would be too easy.

Not that I didn't appreciate the moment...It was strange to witness, her being this comfortable, and vulnerable. I didn't know what to make of it. I didn't know how to handle all the feelings it stirred up in me. I was in too deep, no doubt about it. I wished we could have fallen asleep like this on purpose, but that wasn't in the stars for so many reasons. Even if she wanted a relationship, it wouldn't be with me, her aunt's employee. She'd find herself a Lauren or a Kelli, other rich lesbians who could afford a weekend like this without blinking. But Alison didn't want a relationship. Even here, she was more interested in doing business than taking it easy for a few days.

She mumbled something, and I flinched, afraid she might wake up and chastise me.

Maybe this was the wrong approach. We'd spend a limited time in close quarters. I shouldn't spend that time worrying. I could try to get to know her better. It's what I wanted. It wasn't impossible, right? And then...She might change her mind after all. Here in the dark, with Alison this close to me, I could make myself believe. Wasn't that what Christmas was all about?

Chapter Five

ALISON

After enjoying a deep and undisturbed sleep for more hours than I usually got, I was ready to tackle the day. Not so Cindy who was still deep in dreamland. I cast a fond look at her and got out of bed. The idea of having these magnificent surroundings all to myself for a first cup of coffee filled me with excitement.

Imagine my disappointment when I came downstairs to realize someone else had the same idea.

"Good morning," Marc Frasier greeted me. "I made coffee if you'd like some."

"Later, maybe." This might work to my advantage. I was supposed to enjoy the time off work, but this was an opportunity too good to miss. "Look, if you meant what you said yesterday, we could take the morning to discuss some of the items we scheduled for next year's meeting, move things along."

The offer didn't seem to surprise him.

"I'd like that. How about we combine it with some time on the slopes? Since we're only going to be here a few days..."

Whatever worked. "Why not?"

"Great. I'm sure we can find a quiet corner later for some lunch and signatures. I'm one hundred percent on board with all of your ideas, and I'd like you to start as soon as possible. I only have a few more questions."

"Sounds great to me. Let's do it."

I had a coffee with a muffin after all, got into my winter gear and we headed out.

The stars were aligning. I couldn't believe my luck.

A Christmas getaway, a beautiful woman by my side, my best friends...speechless.

And, even better that mystery guy wasn't some annoying stranger, but Marc Frasier who didn't mind a little work on the side. I knew him well enough. A little small talk, drinks, and skiing, *voilà*, we were in business.

I hadn't lied to Cindy either—I wasn't keen on skiing, but it was a small price to pay, and I enjoyed spending a few hours in the cold crisp air.

"I'm sorry I'm keeping you away from your girlfriend, but I'm glad we came out here," Marc said later when we found a restaurant to have lunch—and finalize some of the paperwork.

To my surprise, I realized his words hit home in a strange way. Perhaps I should have left her a note. She'd be okay, right? In fact, I didn't want her to think that me paying for this trip meant she couldn't have a moment to herself or talk to anyone in the group alone.

I didn't want to be that kind of girlfriend.

It was rather easy to ignore that I wasn't anyone's girlfriend.

"She understands," I said. "Cindy is like me. She loves the work, getting it done, the thrill of the pieces coming together."

"It's great to find someone who completes you like that," he acknowledged. "One can only hope."

Oh, right. Someone had raised his hopes that I could be that person. An awkward silence ensued.

"I'm grateful for her." I meant every word of that—and all of a sudden I had the urge to go back to the cabin and its comforts. I wanted Cindy to know how grateful I was. "I'm glad we got to talk business too, that will give us a good head start for next year."

"No doubt. Are you ready to head back?"

"Sure."

Was I that obvious? Lucky for me he was gracious too. He could do a lot better than being set up by well-meaning friends—him and me both.

CINDY

My awakening wasn't rude, but not the way I hoped it to be either. Alison was gone, her side of the bed cool enough to tell me she'd gotten up a while ago. I wasn't sure how we'd handle breakfast—each to their own? I was hungry, so I reluctantly left the warm covers I now had all to myself and headed for the shower. I assumed Alison would still be here since she had expressed that she wasn't fond of skiing.

My assumption was wrong: When I came into the main area, I found Kelli sipping what seemed to be a hot chocolate in front of the fireplace, like she had announced the day before. There were muted voices from the kitchen area, the others having breakfast. Outside, the sky was a brilliant blue, the snow glistening in the sunlight.

"Hey, good morning," Kelli said. "Isn't it beautiful? I'm not going to move for the next few hours. I don't know when I last had time to read a book."

"I know the feeling. Enjoy."

"Thanks. You're hungry? They just got started over there."

"I'll go take a look, thank you."

I walked over to the kitchen area, all of a sudden self-conscious. I was fairly used to being invisible around privileged people, but I wasn't at work here. I was Alison's guest. Girlfriend.

Jim and Nancy sat at the table, and Lauren stood at the counter, finishing her coffee.

"Cindy, hi, sit with us," Nancy said. "Jim just made a fresh batch of eggs and bacon—for all of us who enjoy taking their time."

"Yeah," Lauren sighed. "My wife is not making it easy on me, sipping her hot chocolate by the fireplace. I might rethink going out...although this might be my last chance. They forecast a snowstorm for tomorrow."

"Where's Alison?"

I realized the question might have been a mistake, because I had three people looking at me with a mix of surprise and sympathy. Not good.

"She and Marc left early this morning."

I summed it up in my mind. My "girlfriend" was out for an activity she didn't enjoy with the guy her friends had intended to set her up with, before they knew about me. Did she try to sabotage the plan? Why? Did she have an interest in him other than getting a deal done? She had told me she wouldn't be opposed to dating women. She hadn't mentioned if dating men had ever been an option. Damn it. It was too early in our "relationship" to be jealous, right?

"Oh, that's right. She wanted to talk to him about business."

It was none of *my* business. Alison paid for my all-inclusive weekend, and in return, I had to be present and keep up the pretense. Easy, wasn't it? If she slipped up, it wasn't my fault.

I helped myself to some coffee and food and sat at the table with them. It surprised me that people like them wouldn't bring their own kitchen staff. So many surprises.

They didn't talk to me except the occasional polite phrase, "Would you like more coffee?" "The sky is really amazing, isn't it?" which was mostly a relief. I was out of my depth. I had to go with what little Alison had told me about these people, nice but too much nagging. They had little to go on when it came to me as well, or maybe they could sense I wasn't the kind of person—rich—they usually hung out with.

I wondered if Alison was enjoying her morning, skiing with Mr. Frasier. It was like a silly romantic comedy, the reluctant heroine lured in by the surprise love interest...How could I be disappointed? I had agreed to take part in a sham.

After breakfast, I started to stack the dishwasher—force of habit.

"You don't have to do that," Nancy said. "Employees from the resort take care of it."

Had I given myself away? Did they ever do these things themselves? Well, Jim made excellent Manhattans and knew how to cook bacon, so that had to count for something.

"I don't mind."

"Alison will be back later, but if you want to take a walk, there are beautiful paths around here. Don't worry, you can't get lost."

"I know something better." Kelli had joined us in the kitchen. "How about you come to the spa with me? I know I said I wouldn't move, but that flight yesterday was something...I could use a good massage."

"There are people who do that here...?" I had gotten ahead of myself. What I meant to ask was, "there's a spa?" but of course there was. This wasn't the kind of cabin people like me imagined. Given that Alison had left me here, why shouldn't I take advantage of the amenities? It wasn't like she had to pay extra. At least I didn't think she'd have to.

"Sure, I'll come with you."

A massage sounded great. It meant no awkward interactions with Alison's friends, and we all could ignore the elephant in the room, so to speak.

Things didn't go as planned.

The employees of the spa were indeed skilled and delivered the perfect massage, but Kelli, I learned, wasn't one to enjoy it in silence.

"If you'd allow me a curious question, when did you and Alison meet?"

Did it matter whether or not I'd allow it? I had to play my part.

"About a year ago, at work." That wasn't a lie. But who talked like that when they were in a new relationship? "Wednesday, December 15th." That, too, was true. I remembered the date. It had no other significance than being the day I had first laid eyes on her, which was highly significant to me. She'd stayed in Mrs. Regan's office for half an hour. I brought in brunch, and then a coffee refill. I'd been thinking about her all day.

I couldn't hold back the sigh, but given I was the recipient of an amazing deep tissue massage, I didn't think my thoughts were that obvious. Or maybe they were.

Kelli chuckled. "I remember the day I met Lauren, too. Trust me, she doesn't. We were really surprised, you know. Alison has never introduced anyone to us."

What did she want me to say to that? You, in return, have introduced plenty of people to her, even though she didn't ask for it?

"We haven't been together that long." It was a good thing I was lying facedown on the massage table so she couldn't see me blush. I wasn't a good liar. That might be why Alison was already regretting bringing me here, because she sensed I had feelings for her. Going skiing with Frasier, when she didn't even like skiing, was that her version of letting me down gently?

"I know, but I mean...Never. She is always working. This was the first time we were able to convince her to stay for the entire Christmas getaway. We were so surprised."

"You invited Frasier so she wouldn't be alone?"

Ouch. That sounded sharper than I'd intended.

Kelli wasn't offended. She laughed. "That sounds bad, doesn't it? But to be honest, we had invited someone else. He couldn't come, and Marc was interested. We didn't even know that he and Alison knew one another, funny how it goes, right? Alison gave us no indication she was interested in women, so this was a surprise. I mean, we're cool with it, obviously. We shouldn't have made any assumptions. She's just so private, we didn't know what to think."

And they couldn't just leave her alone, wait until she was ready? "How long have you known each other?"

"Almost ten years. I worked in her business for a while. I love my job, but wow...She's dedicated. I say that because I love her, otherwise obsessed would be more like it."

I was starting to understand what Alison meant when she said her friends had a little too much of an opinion about her life. Irin had chided me a time or two for always working late and not making enough time for friends and dating. But I, too, loved my job. I was good at it. Why shouldn't I enjoy that? Why shouldn't Alison? Some things were the same, no matter how much money was involved.

"But it must be all different now," Kelli concluded. "Whatever you did to change her mind, thank you. At least we get to spend some time together this year."

"You're welcome," I said.

·♥·♥·♥·♥·♥·

I took a walk by myself later, torn between feeling lonely and disappointed, and sad for Alison because she couldn't seem to make her point, not even with people who claimed to be her friends. Ten years.

And perhaps I wasn't treating her any better, because I so much wished she'd be open to a relationship. With me. How ridiculous was that?

I stole back into the cabin that was now quiet. Everyone had gone out, winter sports, walks, whatever. I went to our room and, after taking a long hot shower, I lay down on the bed, not in the mood to go back to any of my romances. Truth be told I couldn't wait to be home, celebrate Christmas with people who actually wanted me there. The need for denial being greater than anything else, I drifted off to sleep.

"Hey, come on, wake up. Time for cocktails."

I thought I was still dreaming when I opened my eyes and saw Alison standing over me, clad in only a towel.

"Did you have a nice day?"

I sat up, realizing dusk was falling outside. "I guess. What about you?"

Her eyes narrowed at my tone. "It was skiing, but I survived it, and Frasier signed the contract, so there's that. Anything else you wanted to ask?"

"No. Not really."

"All right. You're still coming with me?"

"Yes, of course."

I didn't point out that she wasn't even dressed yet. Alison sighed before she picked up the clothes she'd laid out for herself.

"I could use a drink," she said. "I think you could, too. Give me a minute?"

"Sure. Sorry, I didn't mean—" I was going to launch into an explanation and blame my bratty behavior on not being fully awake when she arrived, but Alison didn't seem to expect one.

"It's fine," she said, ending the subject before she locked herself in the bathroom.

A few days ago, going to a secluded luxurious place with her, nothing to do but relax, seemed like a dream. I wasn't so sure anymore. This setting gave everyone too much time to think. Have regrets. Did I really imagine that she'd be interested, maybe make a pass at me, with her friends around? What had I been thinking?

By the time she returned from the bathroom, I had changed into something more suitable for cocktail time, pulled my hair back into a high ponytail and put on some quick make-up. It would do. Alison, of course, looked flawless in her blouse, pants and heels. I looked down at my little black dress, suppressing a sigh. I was sure every one of them could tell the difference between expensive, and something you'd hope would look the part.

"Come on, girlfriend," Alison said as she took my hand, twisting the knife. I hated to admit Irin might have had a point. Not that Alison was taking advantage—I'd known what I was getting myself into. There was no way I'd escape the predictable heartbreak. I was still mad at her for leaving me here while spending the day with Frasier, regardless of whether I had the right or reason. I was still falling for her, a little more with each moment. I'd play along. I had no choice.

Chapter Six

ALISON

A glass of champagne in hand, music playing softly in the background, I had no reason to be stressed or worried. To the soundtrack of Diana Krall's version of *Have Yourself A Merry Little Christmas*, everything was going as planned. It turned out my friends were highly adaptable to the new reality, and I'd secured an old acquaintance as a new client. The situation could have been a lot more awkward had their original choice made it to the getaway.

Why were my shoulders still tight with tension? Perhaps I should visit the spa too, like Kelli and Cindy had, though I suspected that wouldn't change my state of mind much. I wanted Cindy to enjoy herself while we were here. She had, hadn't she? Kelli was, like the rest of them, easygoing and kind. I couldn't imagine her saying anything that might have upset Cindy—so it had to be me.

I guess there was a reason why I didn't do relationships.

After finishing up a conversation about the next meeting with Marc, I walked over to Kelli who, I realized, had been studying me.

"What is it?" Alcohol and surroundings fortunately contributed to softening my tone.

She raised her eyebrows.

"You never stop for a second, do you?"

I could have misunderstood those words, but I knew where they came from. She cared. They all did. They were driving me crazy. I told her the same thing I had told Marc earlier. At least that wasn't a lie.

"If you must know, I'm taking some more days off for Christmas. What do you all do with that much off time anyway? I'm so glad Cindy understands."

"She really does get you," Kelli said, the truth of her statement filling me with unexpected, inappropriate excitement.

After the weekend, Cindy would be free to do whatever she wanted—be with whomever she wanted. The notion was more uncomfortable than I cared to admit.

"Which is great," she added. "I'll admit we were a bit surprised. She's not who we pictured you with."

"What is that supposed to mean? First of all, I don't appreciate you *picturing* me with anyone..."

The corners of her mouth twitched at my emphasis. I wasn't done, and I wasn't in the mood for humor, not before I had made something clear.

"Why would you be surprised? She's amazing, generous, beautiful...You don't know her at all. She's everything I could ask for." Truth, lie, exaggeration? In any case, she'd been on my mind a lot more than I had realized.

"Whoa, slow down. All I meant to say was she's a bit young."

"Not that much younger," I mumbled. "She works for Aunt Bella."

"Okay. I'm really sorry, I didn't mean to insinuate...You've never introduced anyone to us."

"And now you know why."

We both had to laugh at that, and I was grateful we had avoided a more intense conflict.

"We just kept digging ourselves deeper, weren't we?" Kelli pondered. "Forget I said anything. Forget about the perfect blind date. You figured it out perfectly. Congrats on coming out, and...welcome to the family."

When she hugged me, I didn't feel so self-righteous anymore. Worse, I couldn't be so sure what the truth was any longer.

"Thank you. Seems like the food is arriving...I better find Cindy."

CINDY

The handholding didn't last long. Lauren and Kelli handed everyone glasses of champagne, the toast to family, babies, happy relationships and money barely done when Alison was back in a corner with her business contact. I watched them talk and laugh from afar for a while, then I found myself a seat in a corner where I was hidden by the huge Christmas tree. I only emerged every once in a while for a refill and checking to see if my girlfriend was still busy.

She was.

Earlier today, I'd sympathized with her. I grudgingly wondered if Kelli and the others had a point, if Irin had one too. With Christmas this close, everyone in the mood for celebration, did she really have to finalize this deal now? Except if a business deal wasn't all that was going down...Jim passed me by with a new bottle but turned when he saw me. I held out my glass in utter resignation. I'd never have champagne this expensive again in my life. I might as well take advantage.

Taking advantage...was I? Most of all, I was confused, and lonely...and tipsy. I needed to hold it together. I might not be able to make Alison happy the way I wished to, but I didn't want to embarrass her either. The dinner—catered—came with red wine. Someone had the foresight to seat Marc Frasier at the other end of the table, so the evening was starting to look up. Alison sat next to me, her gaze on me long enough for me to get nervous. *What now*? She leaned in and with a smile, tucked an errand strand of hair behind my ear, her fingers brushing my cheek before she turned to her plate. I sat frozen, feeling my face heat. To an observer, it would look like a casual gesture between lovers. Nothing out of the ordinary. I wanted it to be real more than anything, but it wasn't. If I wasn't careful, I might start to cry.

ALISON

I felt like Cindy had been avoiding me since we came down for dinner, and I was trying to figure out the reason. No, that didn't sound right. I knew the reason, and she was right. I had left her alone for most of the day. It was a bad idea if we wanted to be believable...Come to think of it, it was insensitive. I should have written that note. I wished I could take it back, spend the day with her instead...Marc would have signed the contract anyway. All I wanted was for her to enjoy the weekend in peace after she was already doing me such a big favor...I couldn't fool myself. That wasn't all. I knew better.

"Alison."

I flinched at her quiet tone.

"Would you like me to take those off your plate?"

It took me a few seconds to realize she was talking about the mushrooms that came with the dish. Tonight, we had arranged for a pricey catered gourmet dinner menu, no substitutions. To be honest I should have paid more attention, but it irritated me that my long-time friends didn't remember my aversion. Cindy, however, did. She was that observant.

"No, you don't have to, unless you want them?"

I reached out to lay my hand over hers, relieved that she didn't pull back. With everyone's eyes on us, we had to be believable, right? I wished nobody was looking at us. I wished things weren't this complicated, but that was a lot to hope for even at Christmas time.

"No thanks," she said. "I have a lot."

"The beets are great. And I'll have more of the salad."

For that, I had to let go of her hand. So many regrets. At least, save for the mushrooms, dinner was exceptional, lifting my spirits. That little gesture told me she'd give me a chance to explain myself eventually. We'd be okay.

CINDY

Before dessert, we went on a walk together with the whole group, up to a clearing from which we had a beautiful view of the city below, streetlights, illuminated windows and decorations sparkling in the distance. I looked up and gasped at the sight of the stars.

"Beautiful, isn't it?" Alison said behind me, placing a hand at the center of my back. Maybe she thought we had to be a little more convincing, like when she touched my cheek earlier—or maybe I had leaned back so far she thought I was going to fall over. I didn't appreciate the touch. I didn't even appreciate the stars as much as I should have. So many people would have been grateful for the experience. Why couldn't I be?

It wasn't much of a question really. I knew exactly what was going on, and I had no right to feel this way. We might be pretending, but Alison had never tried to trick me. I was the one who had kept pestering her—we needed more of a story, we needed to be believable. It wouldn't be fair to blame her for trying, would it?

"It is," I agreed. How ironic to be here in these romantic surroundings. Minus the deception, and her friends, this would be my dream come true. We could go home and talk, kiss some more, one thing might lead to—

"Hey, Alison," Jim called from a few feet away. "We need your opinion on something."

Lauren and Kelli stood huddled together, while Jim and Nancy had fallen behind, engrossed in a discussion. Alison cast me a concerned glance.

"Go," I said. "I'm fine."

"This really gets you in the Christmas spirit." I turned around to find Marc Frasier standing behind me, resisting the urge to snap at him for his attempt at small talk. I guess I couldn't blame him either. He'd been set up just as Alison had been, though he didn't need to go skiing with her when he knew her girlfriend was along for the trip. Fake girlfriend, but still.

"It does." Short affirmative answers seemed to be all I was capable of tonight. Too much champagne, food and heartache.

"I wish we could all stay longer," he said. "I don't look forward to being back behind my desk and dealing with all the stressed, impatient people in the city."

"Hm." I hoped that sounded sympathetic enough. "At least you got a head start on that contract."

"Yes, that was a lucky coincidence. Alison is pretty amazing. She knows what she wants."

I wanted her. But that was impossible, no matter how many stars I wished on.

"You've known her a long time?" I asked.

"Long enough to know you're very lucky. You two are great together."

Not that I needed his blessing. He couldn't know that he kept reminding me of the painful truth, so all I could do was politely end the conversation and go find Alison. The night wasn't over yet.

·♥·♥·♥·♥·♥·

Back at the cabin, we sat down with dessert, a white chocolate and cranberry mousse tarte, café and a nightcap. My chagrin aside, I was surprised how quickly the time passed even though all we seemed to do was eat amazing food, drink, sleep and take walks.

"Mistletoe!" Kelli shouted, and I jumped, realizing that I was the one standing underneath the decoration. With Alison. She'd been fairly mellow this evening, but I was sure she was as mortified as I was.

"I'm pretty sure it's holly," Nancy commented. "Doesn't matter. Go ahead."

"Her name is Cindy, and she's gorgeous," Alison declared. "How could I not kiss her?" Before I could prepare myself, she leaned in, private-to-the-point-of-paranoid Alison Carter, in front of her best friends.

This wasn't the first time I had kissed anyone. It might as well have been. Her lips were soft and warm, inviting, irresistible. I might have been trembling a little, a hint of tongue sparking emotions and sensations I shouldn't have in public, or at all. Because we'd both had too much to drink—a drunken joke, that was all it was.

I stepped back, unsure what to do next, unable to handle all the implications of the moment.

I caught Marc Frasier's glance, and thought I'd seen a hint of disappointment. I could sympathize. No, not really. I was devastated.

"I'm getting a headache," I announced. "I think I should lie down for a bit. No," I said to Alison, when she followed me. "You don't have to come. It will go away."

"I don't want to leave you alone," she said softly, probably because everyone was still listening.

I felt too tired to argue. We walked up to the room in silence. After we'd closed the door, Alison asked, "Are you okay?"

What a loaded question. This wasn't the time for that conversation. I wasn't sure there would ever be a time for it.

"I'm just tired. It was a long day."

"True," she acknowledged, sounding relieved. "Did you want to take a bath?"

Was she offering to join me? Why would I even think that? There was no more audience.

I couldn't stop thinking about that kiss, how good, how real it had felt.

"No, I'm just going to take a quick shower."

"Okay, no problem. You can go first then."

I did, and crawled under the covers afterwards, while she took her turn.

I never imagined that pretending would make me this exhausted, but it did. I was awake around three-fifteen, sure Alison was asleep.

She wasn't.

I flinched when I turned around, realizing she was watching me.

"I'm sorry."

"For what? Paying this luxury vacation for me?" I tried to laugh, but it came out strange. "I don't want you to think I'm ungrateful. I could never afford any of this." Whatever happened, it was important to me that she knew.

"I don't think you're ungrateful. This trip, it's no big deal, but that's not the point anyway, is it?"

"Why don't we go back to sleep?"

"You must think I'm a horrible person."

"I don't."

"My aunt is always telling me how smart and competent you are. And kind. She says she doesn't know what she'd do without you."

I didn't feel very kind. In fact, going after Alison in the first place, making her act on a random idea and having too high expectations seemed childish. Perhaps that's what everyone thought I was, a child, or they would if they had any idea of the truth.

"Maybe I should ask for a raise then...the truth is I'm not sure I'm any of those things."

"I think you are. And thank you for going along...with everything. You don't know how much that means to me."

I propped myself up on my elbow, studying her. "You might be right about that. I don't think I get it, why you can't just tell them, but it's not up to me."

Alison didn't argue. "I swear I didn't know Marc was the mystery guy."

"Do you regret bringing me?"

"God, no. That signature was all I ever wanted from him."

The denial was swift, and to my stubborn relief, believable.

"He might have had a different idea."

"Well, that's not my problem. I think he and everyone else got the message."

Yes, but what message?

We were both silent for several minutes. Alison laughed softly.

"I can't sleep. I think too much of a good thing might be the reason. All that food and booze...Would you like to do something crazy?"

She was asking *me*?

"What do you have in mind?" Saying no was rarely on my mind when it came to her, even though I didn't think our conversation had solved anything.

"I haven't had a chance to try the hot tub yet. I'm sure a few minutes would help us sleep. If not, it's fun at least. I don't have time for any of this at home."

"So you know how to relax after all."

I couldn't stay mad at her. Especially if there was the sliver of a chance that she might kiss me again...

·♥·♥·♥·♥·♥·

I had gotten a quick glimpse of the spa area when I went for that massage with Kelli, but the surroundings were even more amazing up close—or sharing them with Alison made all the difference. There was just enough light so we could make it safely into the tub. The huge windows on this side once again lent themselves to wonderful views. Starlight. Why did I have the feeling the universe was mocking me?

Alison wore a bikini, and I didn't know where to look, relieved when we both sat down, up to our shoulders in the swirling warm water. I had brought a black one-piece, adequate for the occasion, not nearly as sexy as hers.

She leaned back against the tile, closing her eyes. I needed to keep my distance. Things were unreal enough already. After this weekend, I'd have to go home, go back to work soon and provide coffee and snacks whenever Alison visited Mrs. Regan. Be polite and efficient.

Keep my distance.

She opened her eyes and looked right at me. I couldn't help myself, couldn't stay away. I think we moved at the same time, though she might have been first.

"I'm sorry," she said.

I wanted to tell her that it didn't matter, that I was a grown-up and could handle rejection like one. We had a deal, one I had agreed to more than once.

That wasn't on her mind though, and if I was honest, it wasn't on mine either. When we kissed again, I understood perfectly what she was apologizing for: There would be no "us" beyond this trip, but she had to know that I couldn't bring myself to give up all hope. I moved even closer, the warmth of her body against mine intoxicating. I might be a grown-up, but I was helpless against the avalanche of sensations, and she had no intention of sparing me, running her hands down my back, pulling me closer. I can't say what this would have led to, had we not heard voices, and the next moment, Lauren said, "Well, that didn't quite work out the way we planned." Kelli stood next to her with a bottle of champagne and two glasses.

"We were just about to leave," Alison said quickly.

"Oh no, you can stay. We'll share, even."

"You shouldn't bring glasses in here anyway."

"Come on," Kelli scoffed. "Who's going to tell?" They didn't seem to mind or care that they'd caught us making out. How Alison felt about it, I wasn't so sure. I cast her a quick glance, but her face was unreadable. Did she regret going that far? What would happen once we were back in the room?

I was going to find out sooner than I'd thought. We both declined the offer of another drink and headed back to our room.

"You have to believe me," Alison told me later, when we were in bed. "I don't know how...I'm sorry. I never meant to make things complicated for you."

"I know."

"No, you don't. I don't have the time for a relationship. It wouldn't be fair to anyone. I just wanted them to stop."

"You don't have to explain it to me. I got it when you did the first time."

"You will find someone who truly appreciates you. More than I ever could."

Oh God, could this get any worse?

"Maybe. Good night, Alison." I turned away, then flinched when she laid a hand on my shoulder. A moment later, the touch was gone.

ALISON

The previous night, I had woken for a few short minutes, realizing that we had somehow closed the space between us, cuddling like two people who were familiar and comfortable with each other. Oblivious. I had felt warm and safe next to her, the silence and warm light created by the falling snow adding to the magical atmosphere.

It wasn't so magical now, and I couldn't feign oblivion any longer.

Confusion was more like it.

After a wonderful day, everything was going downhill—bad metaphor—and all I wanted was to be close to her again. Cindy was mad at me, and perhaps she had reason to be. A few hours hadn't been enough to explain my dilemma after all, before I drew her into this charade, lying to my friends, making her lie to them too.

For what? Because I couldn't make time to come out to them, because I didn't have the courage to tell them that their matchmaking, no matter how well-meaning, bordered on insulting and hurtful?

I'd made my choices.

And someone else got hurt, someone who was most innocent in all of it.

In my mind I replayed the kiss, kisses, under the mistletoe, or holly, who cared? And then again, in the hot tub. I wasn't that cold and heartless—it felt good to share that with someone who was this tender and affectionate, who'd look at me like...damn it. Oblivious didn't even begin to explain it. I should have known better, but I was so caught up in my own problems I couldn't see anything else.

How stupid was I not to realize the reason Cindy had gone out of her way to help me out? It wasn't the lure of a luxury getaway though that probably hadn't hurt. But if I'd told her I had to meet some friends for coffee, she might have come too, be my pretend girlfriend.

I wanted to wake her.

"I didn't mean to hurt you," I whispered, harboring the faint hope that she might be losing sleep like I was.

Her back turned to me, she remained still.

Well, we'd already established I wasn't that courageous. When this was all over, I'd have to apologize to her. Maybe take her out to a nice place again. I could show her around the company if she was interested—that might help her understand what was at stake for me. Aunt Bella sure could give me some pointers on how to proceed.

Content that I wasn't the worst person in the world after all, I slipped back into a restful sleep filled with amazing surprises I'd plan for Cindy.

In my dreams, I kissed her again, too.

Chapter Seven

ALISON

There was something I could do while we were still here though. With renewed resolve, after another good night's sleep, I snuck out of bed while Cindy was still asleep. She looked adorable with her arms around the pillow. I must admit I stood for a few seconds watching her before I took the gift out of my suitcase and put it in the drawer where I could quickly retrieve it later.

When I bought it, I thought it might be part of the gift exchange. Part of the lie. I had changed my mind. After yesterday's events, I didn't want to put Cindy on the spot. I didn't want to wait until tonight.

Lastly, I wanted this to be the beginning of me doing better, being a more considerate person than before. It turned out I cared about what she thought of me after all.

Downstairs, Jim, Nancy and Marc had started breakfast.

I suppressed a yawn as I poured myself a cup of coffee and leaned against the counter.

"So what are everyone's plans for today?" It sounded casual enough to me, but Nancy gave me a knowing smile.

Marc Frasier was a little less observant.

"I know we signed already, but would you be up for going out on the slopes one more time?"

"She looks a little tired," Nancy observed cheerfully. "I think you'll have better luck if you join me and Jim."

"Sure, if that's okay with you, Alison?"

Before I could answer, voices from the other room alerted us to the fact that Lauren and Kelli were on the way, and that Cindy had joined them.

I sat down quickly.

"I think Nancy is right. I'd prefer a slow start today...but you should join them."

"I probably will," he said, smiling at me.

I didn't like that Cindy was catching that interaction, but I was going to make it right. I was determined.

CINDY

Once again, I had woken up alone. This was getting old. I went through my morning routine as quickly as possible, not wanting to give myself too much time to think about what happened last night, and what might have happened.

Where would this end? Did I respect myself enough not to tell her I was ready to try something casual, even if she didn't want a relationship? Could I give her something she might want, or at least appreciate? I didn't know where to start. I was in love with her, had been for a while. Offering to play a part in her plan might have been my worst idea ever.

So much for not over-thinking it.

I met Kelli and Lauren in the main room on their way to breakfast. Lauren gave me a knowing smile. If only she knew...but that was the whole point.

Alison, of course, sat next to Marc Frasier, immersed in a conversation. This, too, was getting old. Her friends didn't have a problem with her being attracted to women, but maybe she had? I thought about how startled she'd been when Lauren and Kelli arrived. She was okay with having lesbian friends, but she wasn't okay with being one? Not that I could complain or judge her. I was the fake girlfriend, tagging along on an all-inclusive trip that she paid for.

I wanted to help her, but I didn't know how. I needed to help myself. I wasn't faring any better on that front.

"Hey, Cindy. I hope you don't mind I started without you. I was so hungry."

Her smile washed all the complications away, for the moment, at least. I was hungry, too, though it was debatable whether food would help. The pastries on the table looked like they'd go a long way to fix any imminent physical needs. If they could fix a confused, soon to be broken heart, remained to be seen.

"It's fine. Thanks for letting me sleep."

A second later, I worried how that might sound to everyone, her in particular...but her smile deepened. "Seemed to me that you needed it." Alison had lowered her voice, though—on purpose?—not enough. Lauren chuckled, and I quickly got up to get myself some coffee.

To my surprise, this time, Alison didn't go out with Marc and the others.

"I think I've had enough of the cold," she said. "I'd rather take advantage of that fireplace today, maybe read a bit. Cindy?"

"Sure," I answered automatically. Why would I disagree with anything? My mind had been wandering in so many directions this weekend, I didn't mind her giving me that—direction. I wouldn't get a lot of reading done, and I didn't think I was supposed to raise certain subjects...I'd be fine. We were going home tomorrow, and I had to brace myself for that.

It was a good thing I had taken care of Christmas presents for my family and friends a while ago. I couldn't imagine myself coming back and having to do the shopping on top of it all.

After everyone, including resort employees that had cleaned up the kitchen, had left the house, it was just the two of us.

We retreated to the sitting area in front of the fireplace.

"Thank God," Alison said. "We have some quiet."

I wasn't sure what to say to that. Did we need it? For what?

"Wait here for me?"

Where would I go? I stood there until she returned with a small gift box. It took me a few seconds to find the right words.

"I didn't think we would exchange gifts..." Try again. "You don't have to give me anything. In fact, I can't accept this after you paid for everything."

"You keep bringing that up. Please, accept it. For bailing me out here, you deserve a lot more. I don't know what I was thinking, dragging you into this." She shook her head with a self-conscious laugh. "Put me out of my misery?"

I finally took the box from her and opened it. The necklace inside was beautiful and I knew immediately it cost a lot more than I wanted to know. I counted five gemstones on the snowflake pendant. I was sure they were diamonds.

"Alison." It was hard to tell whose misery was greater—or who was more pathetic. I didn't want expensive gifts. I couldn't care less about the spa, and the champagne...

"Please. It's what I can do."

I stepped forward, and reluctantly, she let herself be embraced. My own hopes might be clouding my view, but I didn't want to let go. I wanted a space in which neither of us had to pretend. If only for Christmas.

"Then let me thank you."

This time, I initiated the kiss, and she didn't try to stop me. Instead, she pulled me closer, deepening it. The rush of desire made my knees weak. We'd be alone for a few more hours...That seemed to be on her mind too, because her hands wandered underneath my sweater, hot on my skin. A sound of pure bliss escaped my lips. Between heated kisses, I started to unbutton her shirt, eager to caress the soft skin revealed.

Alison took a step backwards, regarding me with a mix of regret and an affection so deep it made me hopeful nonetheless. Once more, I waited.

"I want to," she whispered. "But not here, not rushed like this. You deserve better."

I could barely breathe when the meaning of her words sank in. Did she just say we had a chance, that there might be a future for us beyond this weekend?

I couldn't tell her that after all the time I'd lusted for her, it felt hardly rushed—but I understood it did for her. I still didn't understand everything, except that I wanted to be close to her, and for once, she didn't seem to mind.

We sat down on the couch, and she pulled me into her arms, her hand gentle in my hair. I shivered from the sheer pleasure, or maybe the memory of moments ago.

She leaned in to kiss me softly.

"I know I've told you many times about how I love my job..."

But? There might be room for something—someone—else? Even if that someone was far out of her league? She had already introduced me to her friends. She said she wanted me too. Didn't she? She said I deserved better, and perhaps she was right to point out the timing was questionable.

There was no one better for me than her.

"And I do, but there's always someone out there waiting for you to fail, so they can move into your space. I haven't felt this safe in ages. Thank you for that."

My guard wasn't just down, it was gone as I breathed in her scent. I couldn't help myself, even though Alison was still talking about the job.

"It doesn't have to end." She didn't answer, which I chose to see as encouragement. "I mean, we live in the same city. You have to eat sometime…We could figure this out. We could make the time."

"Cindy," she whispered. "You don't know me at all."

"Only one way to change that."

With a sigh, she tightened her arms around me. "This, right now, it's something good. Let's leave it at that."

Alison was right when she said we didn't know each other well, but the same went for everyone at the beginning of a relationship, didn't it? We had a certain…compatibility. That was a good start. It would be different if she didn't like me at all, but I didn't get that from her. I would make her stop worrying about what she could give to me and make her see that I already had everything I wanted.

I had thought that the environment would make everything easier, but the luxury trip and the friends might be the biggest distraction. We could make time for each other once we were home.

ALISON

I stopped arguing, because time was too precious. Soon, the cabin would be filled with kind and nosy people again—who would probably make assumptions as to what had happened while they were away.

As usual, I had been the oblivious one, to my own feelings, to how far we'd taken this already.

I'd meant to give her something nice, to make sure she knew I appreciated her. I didn't mean to lead her on. I didn't want to disappoint her.

"I know I'm repeating myself, but it doesn't have to be complicated," she whispered. "We can figure this out."

It was going too fast. I loved being close to her, holding her. We were so comfortable we almost drifted off to the sounds of the crackling fire.

Looks could be deceiving. Too much still stood between us. There was nothing to figure out. I needed to stop indulging myself. I was only going to hurt her more, and that had never been the plan.

"Perhaps."

Fortunately, that seemed enough for her. She leaned in for another kiss when we heard the sound of keys.

"They're back," Cindy said, looking alarmed all of a sudden. "What's the story? Is there a story?"

"We already have a story," I reminded her as I straightened my shirt and buttoned it a little higher. "Don't worry."

"Okay." Cindy didn't sound too convinced. She, too, tugged on her clothes, studying me. I nearly started to fidget.

Too fast, too much.

"What's the matter?" I tried to keep my tone light, for her sake, for mine. I was beginning to look forward to being home, back at work where things were simple and logical, not like the mess I created.

"You'll remember what I said, right? I'm not trying to make this complicated for you, but...you seem to like me."

That was an understatement. I hoped she knew that.

"I like you too. A lot. We can take all the time we need once we're back home."

I wished that were true, but time was running out on us, because this was nothing more than a Christmas fantasy.

The sounds of laughing and chatting in the hall put an end to it, and seconds later, we were no longer alone.

Chapter Eight

CINDY

I n the afternoon everyone was getting ready for cocktails again. I vowed to take it easy on the alcohol, drunk enough on emotion. Observing Alison, I was starting to see her in a new light. I shouldn't have been so hard on her for being polite to Frasier, and building a friendly rapport to get that contract signed. She'd spent the afternoon with me, not him.

Irin would have to admit I'd been right to take a chance on Alison. We would figure it out. I couldn't keep the smile off my face as my mind kept going back there.

"So, how are you all going to do Christmas?" Nancy asked when we sat around the table. "I am gaining weight just thinking about all those dinners coming up."

"We'll have everyone over at once," Lauren said. "My mom, Kelli's parents, siblings with kids, a few cousins and friends...and then we'll head to New York for New Year's Eve."

"That sounds amazing," Frasier commented. "I'll take my parents and my sister for dinner, but I'll be working most of the time. What about you, Alison?"

"Same here. I'll have to catch up."

Kelli shook her head. "I'm sure Cindy will have something to say about that. You're not going to leave her home alone the whole time?"

"No, I'm not." Alison sounded a bit impatient, but she smiled when she looked at me and took my hand. She hadn't told me anything about her family. I imagined her meeting mine for Christmas dinner. I loved the idea, even though it wasn't realistic under the best of circumstances.

Later, when everyone retreated to their rooms, she stayed, so I did too. Alison looked pensive, and I wondered if the conversation about family was the reason.

"I told my parents I was going on a trip with friends," I confessed. Not that she'd asked.

"Well, it will be all over soon, and I suppose they won't press you on details."

"Are you going to see yours?"

"They both passed away. Seven and ten years ago."

"I'm sorry."

"Don't be. They were good people, and I have amazing memories. I don't get depressed at Christmas. I did my grieving." Her calm, but firm tone told me that this wasn't the night to deepen the subject. I didn't.

"I'll have to go to the office too... This was the first time I took a vacation this close to the holidays."

"You know that I talked to Bella. She's aware that it's all my fault."

"She didn't use those words, but yes, I know she was okay with it."

"So you don't have to worry about a thing. You can go home and no one will know you were my pretend girlfriend."

I'm sure she didn't mean for those words to sting, but they did. Looking up, I realized I wasn't the only one they'd hurt when I saw Lauren standing a few feet away. Neither one of us had noticed her come in, but she must have overheard what Alison had said. Her disappointment was palpable.

"What the hell does that mean?" she asked.

Alison flinched, but she straightened when she said, "Nothing. We all have an early start tomorrow. Let's go to bed, Cindy."

"No, wait a second. I thought we were your friends. What are you talking about?"

"I should leave you alone..." I offered, but Lauren shook her head. "No, Cindy, it seems like you were in on the joke. Pretending to be gay, really? I didn't expect that from you, Alison."

"I'm not pretending to be anything," Alison said coolly.

"You're not? Why make us believe you two were together?"

Because we are, I wanted to say. *Well. Almost.* I stayed quiet, already feeling guilty.

"Because it's so much better than the alternative," Alison shot back.

"I don't get what you're saying."

"You really don't, do you? All the time, telling me I needed to work less, to meet someone, sad alone Alison who couldn't get laid."

I saw Lauren's jaw drop slightly. "No one ever said that."

"Not in those words, but you all had too much fun pushing those guys on me. It wasn't fair to them either, because one or two were actually looking for a relationship."

Lauren had some of the same questions I had.

"What am I missing? I'm sorry we tried to set you up a time or two, but if you weren't into guys, you could have just said so.

Do you think any of us would have judged you for that? Kelli and I? That is hurtful."

"So was making me think I could never be enough of my own, that there was something wrong with me because I liked my job and what it got me. It's how I want to live. I'm sorry. No, actually, I'm not. I never wanted to be in a relationship." She fled upstairs before Lauren could answer.

"I am sorry," I offered.

Lauren shrugged. "I don't blame you." That sounded almost like she pitied me, and maybe I deserved that. Talk about hurtful. Alison's parting words felt like a physical blow, even though I knew they were meant for Lauren more than they related to anything that had happened between us. Or was I just fooling myself, again?

"I think I should..." I started.

She made a dismissive gesture. "Sure. Whatever. I just came here to get my book."

When I arrived upstairs, the room was already dark. I was both frustrated and relieved. Avoiding uncomfortable subjects was what had gotten us here, but I didn't think I could handle any more hits either, intended or not.

The next morning would be awkward. I didn't think Lauren would keep a secret this big from her wife.

I grabbed my PJs and some underwear and retreated to the bathroom for a few minutes. By the time I got into bed, I had found some last shreds of hope to cling to.

We had created a mess, but what if something better could come out of it? At least the truth was out.

"At least you two started talking," I said in the darkness. "I'm sure they'll all understand eventually."

"I'm sorry, Cindy. I really don't want to go over this again. Let's sleep."

Things might look different in the light of day.

I still felt bad about leaving everybody to think I might be a careless gold digger, and their friend had lied to them days before Christmas. Not that the timing mattered.

Alison had been hurting, more than anyone knew. They needed to clear the air, even though I wouldn't be part of the process.

Against all odds, I still hoped I could see her once we were back home.

Chapter Nine

CINDY

As predicted, breakfast passed with a lot of meaningful looks and a few jibes. Alison pretended not to notice. I cringed every time.

Marc Frasier clearly had no idea what was going on, but I didn't have it in me to feel petty about it this morning. I couldn't mention anything either, because those weren't my friends, and the only thing they knew about me was that I'd lied to them on Alison's behalf. Not that I had said so much that wasn't true.

I still wanted to make it true. That wasn't good enough.

The sky was cloudy, fitting my mood perfectly. It had started to snow, and the arrival of the shuttle was still about an hour away. I hoped we wouldn't get stuck here.

"You guys have a great Christmas," Nancy said. "We'll call all of you after the big party." She hugged everyone, including me, though she gave me the same look Lauren had the other night.

I felt like I should have corrected the record and told them Alison hadn't dragged me into anything. I let the moment pass, and then the shuttle arrived, and we were on our way to the airport.

The couples talked among themselves in hushed tones, which left Frasier to try and make some small talk that neither I nor Alison were interested in. Eventually, he gave it up.

When the bus lurched slightly, I looked outside, my jaw dropping. When we'd left, a few snowflakes had been dancing merrily. Those snowflakes had multiplied.

Kelli's gaze was following mine. "Yeah, I hope that's not going to get worse. I don't want to be stuck in the airport."

That was the last thing I wanted, with so many thoughts to sort out. I was still worried Alison might blame me because the secret got out. I was worried she might never want to see me again. No, if I was honest, I already knew. I needed to get home in order to get my head out of the clouds. Pretend nothing had ever happened.

I, the miracle worker, had no idea how to do that. I guess I was only good at solving problems when they weren't my own.

We quickly went from the freezing drop off zone into the airport building and found our respective gates.

To no surprise, Alison found herself an outlet for her tablet and called up some files.

"Would you like a snack?" I asked. Start with something easy.

"We just had breakfast," she said, looking up quickly before she dropped her gaze back to her screen. "But if you want something, go ahead." More caffeine and sugar, especially considering airport prices, wasn't the best idea, but I didn't want to sit and watch her work either.

I went to get myself a coffee and a donut and sat in the seat next to her. I wanted to talk to her. I wasn't sure what I was going to say, if an apology would change things, but I never had the chance.

The display of the schedule changed to announce that all flights for the next few hours were either delayed or canceled. A quick check confirmed that ours fell into the latter category.

"Alison."

"I know we need to talk. I don't think this is the right—"

"Alison, please. Look."

This would be the first time I heard her mutter an expletive under her breath.

"I know, but there's nothing we can do about it. The weather's getting worse."

"No kidding." She leaned back in her seat with a sigh. "Just what I needed. Given what this all cost, they should give us a hotel room for free."

"I am really sorry. This is all my fault." I might have been overreacting, a bit melodramatic from the emotional roller-coaster I couldn't seem to get off of. "I should have never gone along with any of this."

"Cindy, stop."

"You wouldn't be in this mess with your friends if you had just gone alone, and you paid a ton of money on top of it. I'm sorry." I was also tired and unhappy, because I had made myself the center of a ridiculous plan, and this was how it had worked out. Alison might have paid for everything, but I still had loaded my credit card in a futile attempt to look appropriately wealthy next to her...Not that anyone cared. They cared that we had told them lies.

"Cindy. None of it is your fault." She turned and hugged me, probably feeling sorry for me. That was even worse. "I'm not sure how I can make this right, or make you see I'm not that horrible person I've been this weekend. But I think we should get out of here. I'll see what I can do. Wait here?"

There wasn't much of an alternative. Fortunately, the people around us were too occupied with their own phones to notice what was going on.

Alison went to the counter of our airline. I could only see her from the back, but the employee looked apologetic. Did that mean we might have to spend the night here? I wasn't sure at this point what I wanted, to be with her, to be by myself, have a chance to deal with all those conflicting emotions. I'd been in love before, had relationships not work out. I'd survive. I didn't need to make it such a big deal, did I?

She returned, giving me a smile that was probably meant to be reassuring.

"Good news and bad news. We're not going to get out of here before tomorrow, but they'll pay. Let's go check in?"

"I'm sorry," I said, standing up. I was sounding like a broken record, getting on my own nerves.

"You have to stop saying that. Unless you had something to do with all that snow, I won't blame you. And honestly, it might be a good thing."

She didn't elaborate, and I didn't ask. We could stop pretending, right? But what lay ahead, would probably be nothing like my Christmas dreams.

·♥·♥·♥·♥·♥·

"This is better than I thought it would be," Alison said when we walked into the hotel room. I cast a look outside the window. I could barely see anything in what was now a full-on blizzard. Fortunately, we'd been able to go from the airport to the adjacent hotel building without ever going outside, and this room looked like a place where privileged folks could easily spend a few hours in transit. One king-sized bed though. Why wasn't I surprised?

"Are you mad at me?" I asked. The answer was still of utter importance to me.

"Why would I be mad at you?" She hung her coat in the wardrobe and sat in one of the armchairs. "Look, you're right in one thing, this was a pretty bad idea to begin with, but here we are. I'm not the one that's mad, but I'd understand if you were. I know I'll have a lot of explaining to do, exactly what I wanted to avoid. Maybe I could have avoided it. I can't go back now."

"They are not completely innocent in this. I'm sure they'll understand."

"Yeah, maybe. I am sorry too. I didn't imagine any of it to go the way it did."

Including yesterday afternoon, I was sure. I felt like crying, but I wasn't going to do it in such close proximity. I didn't think she was a horrible person. I was mad, not at her, but the timing and the circumstances that were so very wrong for us.

"You have a big family?" she asked.

I found it hard to follow all those twists and turns.

"I mean, you'll have a big Christmas party?"

"Two siblings with spouses, one nephew and my parents," I said. "Not that big. Do you have any siblings that you'll see?"

She shook her head.

"I might have dinner with Bella and her husband and spend the rest of the time in the office. Don't pity me. I chose this."

"I wasn't going to. When Nancy calls, tell her it was all my idea, that you were tired of being set up, and overreacted a bit. It's more important that they forgive you than me."

"I'll figure it out. I don't really want to think about it now." Alison got up, speaking as she walked across the room to where I was still standing at the door. "I don't want to think about any of it." When she pulled me to her, I had nowhere to go. There was nowhere else I wanted to be, her arms around me, her lips on mine soft and warm.

A sweet and too short moment later, she stepped back, the conflicting emotions written all over her face.

"I'm sorry. I shouldn't have done that. It won't happen again."

How I wished she didn't mean it.

"Yes, I know. You don't have the time or inclination. I guess I'll have to spend the rest of the evening with one of the three best-selling lesbian romance novels. I can offer you one too."

"You *are* mad."

"I'm not. It's just a little hard to go back to fiction after...everything."

"Believe me, I know what you mean. Are you hungry?" Alison asked.

"Sure." I might indulge her, but it had been a while since the last meal.

We ordered room service for dinner, with a bottle of wine. Outside, the snow had calmed down and eventually stopped falling, the moonlight casting a romantic light.

She'd told me she felt safe with me. The feeling was mutual. It seemed that for a few moments, all of our worries, ambitions and fears of being judged one way or another, didn't count.

It would be childish to assume it could always be that way.

"You are such an amazing person," Alison said, her eyes bright from emotion and wine. "You'll find someone who deserves you."

All this talk about deserving made me uncomfortable. Maybe all these complications were what we deserved for lying. Maybe I was failing to make her understand that she deserved to be loved.

"What about you? Don't you think there's somebody out there who'll understand? Your dedication to the job, and your need for privacy?" And why couldn't I be that person?

"Is that what it is?" She laughed wistfully. "Maybe they are all right, and I cut myself off from feeling something. Especially around the holidays."

"It's normal when you miss someone."

"But I've told you, I worked through all of that. I just really don't think friends should meddle in your private life. And I do love my job, even if it's demanding and doesn't leave much time for anything else. Sometimes it's worth it, you know?"

"I know. I mean I'm not that wealthy, but getting the job at your aunt's company was a dream come true. And it enabled me to load my credit card to buy my wardrobe for the weekend."

"You didn't need to do that. Did you see Nancy and Jim's ugly Christmas sweaters?"

"I did. I assumed they were the rich people's equivalent of ugly Christmas sweaters."

"Oh Cindy."

I couldn't help it, not when she was looking at me that way.

"You'd only need to make one little change. You wouldn't have to give up anything…I don't take up a lot of time and space, I promise. I just want to be with you."

"You are too sweet. That's exactly why we shouldn't go there. I'll disappoint you soon enough."

"We'll see about that."

I, too, was tipsy and sentimental, and a heartbeat away from begging.

"Believe me," she said. "It's better that way. You'll find that person."

I wanted to beg. I also wanted to shake her—but even in my confusing state between bliss and misery, I understood that there were still missing pieces to uncover.

"I'm not going to sleep on the couch," I declared.

"Neither will I. We're adults, right?"

Who was she trying to convince?

That night, each of us stayed on her side of the bed, no intentional or unwitting transgressions. The dream was coming to an end. Happy endings were for romance novels.

Chapter Ten

CINDY

After the last flight, we said goodbye at the airport. I put on a brave face though the reality of the moment was starting to hit me. The end. The long weekend had come and gone, and I had failed to convince Alison that we could have something real.

The cab driver was listening to Christmas music, not engaging save for asking for my destination, and, once we'd reached it, the fare.

I felt exhausted, and numb at the same time, climbing the stairs to my apartment. For a split-second, I thought about doing laundry, then abandoned the idea and made some coffee. When it was done, I took my cup and a plate of cookies from the pantry to the living room and turned on the TV.

A Christmas romance had just ended, another one began. A marathon.

I could feel the tears forming behind my eyes. I had done everything wrong. There was no do-over for me.

The phone rang. I considered not answering, but it was Irin who must have had a sixth sense.

"You can say 'I told you so,'" I sniffed. "You were right about everything."

"Oh sweetie, I would never say that. What happened?"

"It's over," I said, and maybe that wasn't true either—how could it be over if everything was fake to begin with?

"I'm so sorry. Should I come over?"

I considered her offer. Everything was still too raw. Perhaps I wanted to dwell a little—and I was so, so tired.

"That would be great," I said. "I have coffee, cookies, and wine."

"Sounds perfect. I'll be right there."

ALISON

On the cab ride home from the airport, I considered going straight to my office but decided against it. I went there early the next morning at a time when most of the shops in the area were still closed. It was perfect to catch up on messages and notes left in my absence—and the perfect distraction, until I found an email from Marc Frasier. He ended it with *Merry Christmas to you and Cindy!*

I sat back, scenes from the weekend flashing in my mind. Her, on the plane next to me, studying me as if she needed to prepare for a test. Putting on make-up as we got ready for yet another cocktail hour, always by my side, going along with my ridiculous plan. The way she'd kissed me...not part of the charade, it had never been for her.

And I? Was I really that selfish—or confused? It was too late to worry about that. I had pushed her away, again and again.

At least, no one would ever try to set me up with a nice guy again. The truth was out. I had my freedom back.

I had everything I wanted, didn't I? But if that were true, I wouldn't have so many regrets.

CINDY

I rin stayed until late that evening, and she came over the next night as well, shared dinner with me, and listened. To my relief, Mrs. Regan wasn't at the office on my first day back. However, the next day, which was also my last before the holidays, she came in early.

"Good morning, Cindy."

I wish she wouldn't be quite so cheerful.

"Could you get us some coffee and something sweet? There are a few items I'd like us to discuss before we resume next year."

"Yes, of course, Mrs. Regan."

I was afraid she would ask me how my "collaboration" with Alison worked out, but fortunately the day turned out to be much too busy. We had various meetings to discuss upcoming projects with teams, and I had a multitude of notes to take and organize. There would be no need for a guilty conscience—I more than made up for the time I'd taken off.

"Happy Holidays," she said, handing me an envelope when we had finished the last meeting. "I'll see you next year."

"Happy Holidays, Mrs. Regan."

I gave my desk a last cursory glance. I was putting on my coat when the door opened, and Alison walked in. She froze for a second, and so did I.

"Cindy, hi," she said. "I just came here to see Bella."

"I assumed."

"Merry Christmas. Enjoy your time off." I didn't believe that she meant to be cruel, so I let it slide, even though the moment was hardly as painful for her. I couldn't help staring. As usual, she was impeccably dressed, her scarf fashionably draped over her coat. No hat. Snowflakes were melting in her hair that fell on her shoulders in soft waves. I knew from memory how soft it was...but that was all forbidden territory now.

"Are you coming in, Alison?"

Mrs. Regan stood in the doorway, looking amused. "And Cindy, why are you still here? Didn't you have a date?"

I blushed hotly while Alison used the moment to get inside her aunt's office. She sat with her back to me. Mrs. Regan waved and closed the door, and I finally left, my eyes welling up.

ALISON

"**W**hy did you have her work this late?" I complained.

This wasn't how I had meant to greet Aunt Bella, but I was still shaken. I had asked to meet her this late to make sure Cindy wouldn't be in the office.

"Well, not that it's any of your business, but she just took a few days off as you know. We had a few things to finish up. What's with the bad mood?"

I glanced at my hands, remembering telling her that I'd need Cindy for a project.

"I'm sorry," I muttered.

"That's all right, though I think there might be someone who needs an apology from you."

"You talked to Jim and Nancy."

Aunt Bella made a dismissive gesture. "I did, but they know what they contributed to the situation. They've been on your case for years, and while they didn't appreciate being lied to, they can understand why you did it."

"Oh, good. I was going to call them."

"Shouldn't you call Cindy first?"

I shook my head. "We said everything we needed to. She knows I'm sorry for putting her in that position."

"Are you?"

"What do you mean? Of course I am. But she'll be all right. She'll find someone."

I might have been more convincing if my words didn't sound slightly bitter. A date, Bella had said. Was Cindy already seeing someone else?

"You don't seem happy about that prospect."

I valued her friendship and advice, but tonight I couldn't handle the way she saw right through me. I got to my feet.

"I'm sorry, I forgot something. In any case, I just wanted to tell you I'll be pretty busy in the coming days, preparing the project for Marc and all, but I'll join you and Harry for Christmas Eve dinner. I'll see you then?"

I didn't wait for an answer.

I had lied again. There was nothing immediate I needed to take care of. I headed home past windows decorated for the holidays, the scents, sounds and sights of Christmas everywhere. Knowing that no one and nothing was waiting for me bothered me, for the first time that I could remember.

CINDY

The weather had calmed down, only a few flurries forecast between now and Christmas. Salt and pebbles crunched under my boots when I walked to the coffee shop where I was meeting Irin today. It was almost empty, the usual suspects off for the holidays.

Irin wasn't there yet, so I ordered a specialty coffee and found myself a table in the corner and opened the envelope, feeling my jaw drop. I had somewhat expected a bonus after all the time I put in, but I had no idea it would be this high. I wouldn't have to worry about my credit card bill any longer.

Sipping the sweet beverage, I thought of Alison. She wasn't all wrong. I was proud of what I'd achieved, and it did take hard work. I still didn't get why that should be all.

I missed her so much.

I was mad at her, because she had made it pretty clear that we'd go back to friendly interactions at Mrs. Regan's office, concerning pastries, coffee, maybe a glass of juice?

Alison had never said it in so many words, but perhaps she truly believed that loving someone, being in love, was a waste of time.

I couldn't spend the rest of my life obsessing over these questions, but I knew I would be for some time to come.

The song playing in the background ended. The next one was *Please Come Home for Christmas*, and when Irin finally arrived, she found me close to tears once more. This had to stop, especially now that we were in public.

"What happened?"

"I ran into Alison at the office," I said.

In the past couple of days, I had given her more than enough context. Irin put her own beverage on the table and sat across from me, looking pensive.

"That's got to be hard. But it's bound to happen again, right? She works on projects for your boss?"

"Oh crap. Now I'll have to find a new job too." If that was a bit melodramatic, I didn't care. I was seriously considering the idea. "I'm such a fool."

Irin shook her head. "No. You're just in love."

I wasn't sure if there was any significant difference between the two.

·♥·♥·♥·♥·♥·

As I was getting ready to celebrate Christmas at my parents' house, I told myself that I had no reason to feel this deeply melancholic. I had to put on a brave face, because there was no way I'd explain to everybody that I had done this foolish pretense with a woman who couldn't bring herself to follow her heart.

No, there was no good way to do that. In front of the mirror, I hesitated, then I put on the necklace. I probably should have given it back, but it seemed like this would be all I'd ever have to connect me to this complicated, magical weekend.

The cab driver honking jolted me out of my musings, and, juggling gift bags and my keys, I went downstairs.

ALISON

Not much the wiser on anything, but grateful not to be alone for a few hours, I rang Aunt Bella's doorbell at 4:00 p.m. on Christmas Eve. I had put off the conversations with my best friends, just exchanged a few holiday greetings via text. I did call Marc on the phone because that was easy, and we had business in the near future after all.

Clutching a bottle of Bella and Harry's favorite Scotch and a bouquet of seasonal flowers, I waited until they opened the door to me, smiling and happy to see me.

I wondered if Cindy was bringing her date to see her parents—or had I misunderstood something? I didn't want to think about it now, or ever.

"Come on in," Harry said. "You're just in time for appetizers. I made mini quiches."

He loved cooking. Come to think of it, he never seemed to have a problem with Bella spending so much time at the office. That kind of relationship was obviously possible...for some people. I pushed the thought aside once more and forced a smile.

"I can't wait."

Once we sat down with wine and appetizers—mini quiches were only the beginning—Harry asked me, "It's been a while since we had you here. How have you been? Bella told me you went on a trip with Jim and Nancy?"

There was no escape. "Yes. We had a great time."

"And you secured a client."

"What else did she tell you?" I asked, my tone sharper than intended. "I'm sorry. I guess I'm still winding down from everything...this year, actually. It's been busy."

"We understand. And Christmas isn't always the easiest time."

I didn't want to get into that either, though I had to remember I wasn't the only one in the room missing someone.

"Yes, but still you made time to harbor me. Thank you."

"We are happy to," Bella said. "Since we already started, how about we continue the gifts? Harry and I have something for you."

While my life hadn't always been like that, money wasn't a problem these days, and I enjoyed spending it on the people I loved. Bella and Harry, my friends—if I still had any. I ignored the image that flashed in my mind.

Along with the "thanks for having me" gift I had bought them tickets for the opera, something I knew they both loved, best seats in the house. They gave me expensive chocolates along with a scarf from my favorite designer—not cheap either.

Even surrounded by all this privilege, I couldn't stop melancholy from creeping in. What was it all worth? A few hours from now, I would be back in my condo, by myself.

Yes, I loved my job, and I was looking forward to the new year, new projects, happy clients.

Until then, I'd have to find something to do.

I joined Bella in the kitchen where she was making coffee, studying me intently as she went. I had a hard time not fidgeting.

"Cindy Jeffries is a remarkable young woman."

"I never said otherwise. And I will apologize for dragging her into this, just because I couldn't tell my friends they were out of line."

"You're sure that is all?"

"I know what you're trying to do, but—"

"You're busy. You've dedicated all of your time and energy to your company, and you thought it was always going to be this way."

Was she trying to make me cry? I didn't want to be reminded that the one time things might have been different, I'd screwed up, badly.

"It will always be this way. I'm fine with it."

"Alison," she held my gaze, "people are allowed to change their minds."

I understood it was important to Bella to make her point. I couldn't go there, not on this day, after everything I'd said to Cindy.

"I think the coffee is ready." She sighed, but let me off the hook, and we went back to the dining room. For the rest of the evening, we left delicate subjects alone.

When I got ready to leave, Aunt Bella picked a small envelope from the Christmas tree before she and Harry saw me to the door.

I hadn't seen until now that my name was on the envelope.

"There's one more thing," she said, handing it to me.

"Oh no," I said. "You've already given me so much."

"All we want is for you to be happy. I'd like you to open this later."

"Now I'm scared...curious, I mean."

She laughed, sharing a personal look with Harry.

"Have a good night. And I promise, there's no reason to be afraid. None at all."

If only this were true...

CINDY

My sister Mona greeted me at the door with a hug and then helped me get the bags into the living room and under the tree. A huge amount of packages was already waiting, most of them for my three-year-old nephew Jack, I supposed.

"It's a good thing the snow finally stopped for a bit," she said. "Brett and I were worried about the roads. How was your trip?"

"Really nice," I said. That's all anybody needed to know.

"So you had a good time?" Mom asked. One by one, everyone was joining us in the living room. Brett handed me a glass of wine. Dad arrived to give everyone a refill, and Tim and his husband Cory followed with Jack in tow.

"Yes, it was amazing," I answered between hugs after placing the glass on a side table. "I'm so glad to see you all."

I was. This was real, spending the holidays with people who knew me and loved me for who I was. Maybe I had judged Alison harshly, but she'd felt that by telling her friends the truth, she'd disappoint them. My coming out or my work hours weren't under scrutiny here, never had been.

If only she could realize that perhaps the problems she saw didn't exist, but I didn't know what I could have done differently to make her understand that. She was smart and successful...who was I wanting to change her perspective on anything? Except...We'd had a real connection, one I couldn't think about now.

"That is a beautiful necklace," Mona said. "Was there anyone special on that trip with friends?"

I reached for my glass and took a hasty sip, coughing. She laughed, patting my back. "I see."

"No you don't. Can't a woman just buy a nice piece of jewelry for herself?"

"She can, but no offense, I don't think you'd spend two months worth of rent on a necklace."

I gulped. Of course I'd known it was expensive, but this much?

"Stop it, she doesn't want to tell you," Tim said, and I gave him a grateful smile. "Is she coming to the party?"

"Oh, come on."

Fortunately, Jack had discovered the cat curled up under the tree, and in an instant, all the adults were more occupied with keeping the tree from falling on child and feline than the origin of my necklace.

Thank you, Jack.

Outside, the flurries had become rain, and then freezing rain by the time we were halfway through appetizers. None of us lived far away, so that wouldn't be a problem, though I was pretty sure guest rooms had been set up.

To be honest, I'd prefer staying to going back to my empty apartment, even though I was still too self-conscious to share the whole story with anyone other than Irin.

ALISON

I sat in the back of the cab, envisioning a hot bath with a nightcap, and maybe a couple of the chocolates that were part of my gift. We drove past houses displaying every imaginable Christmas motif, the scenery looking happy and inviting despite the harsh weather. Multiple cars in driveways, visitors from near and far.

There was no point in wondering what Cindy was doing at this moment, but I couldn't help it. Was she happy surrounded by family? Was she still thinking of me at all?

I had made a decision for both of us, and I'd have to live with the consequences.

Since we were only a few blocks away from my building, I reached into my purse for my wallet, feeling the envelope Aunt Bella had given me. Why did she want me to wait to open it? Curious, I couldn't wait any longer and tore it open.

Inside was a piece of paper. My jaw dropped when I read what was written on it, my eyes prickling all of a sudden. I took a deep breath.

"Change of plans," I said out loud. "We're going to 5932, Gardenia Road."

The cab driver was unfazed by my announcement. "As you wish," he said, and, at the next corner, turned the car around.

CINDY

We were about to start dinner when the doorbell rang. Dad was still occupied carving the turkey, and dishes were handed from one person to the next.

For a split-second, a foolish, unreal hope took over my mind, just as Dad said, "Can't be the neighbors. They went to visit their kids. I'm sure someone's car broke down."

"That's okay," Brett commented. "That turkey is big enough for a few more."

"I'll get it," I offered.

"Thank you, Cindy."

I walked to the front door, opened it and froze, not just because of the cold coming in.

Alison stood there, shivering, arms wrapped around her middle.

"Hi, Cindy."

For a moment, I was afraid that if I moved or said anything, she'd disappear again. Then I noticed that her coat and hair were wet.

"Please, come in already."

Alison hesitantly stepped inside.

"You can take off your coat." She did as I said but held on to it. "I can show you somewhere you can dry your hair. You don't want to get a cold on this day of all..." I stopped rambling and asked the all-important question. "What are you doing here?" I wasn't one hundred percent sure I wanted to know, because the answer would not be what I wanted it to be. No way. She had said it would be better if we forgot all about it.

Because I could do better.

Because she...who knew?

She showed me a piece of paper, written on it, *Ken and Marsha Jeffries, 5932 Gardenia Road.*

I looked back at Alison, still dumbfounded.

She laughed softly. "Aunt Bella must have gotten this address from your HR file. She gave it to me as a Christmas present. I guess she thought I needed a bit of a push."

To do what? My heart was about to beat out of my chest.

"I'm sorry. I know it's Christmas Eve and you're with your family, but can we talk?" she asked, now sounding serious and sober.

I had made so many offers. I couldn't imagine what else we needed to talk about, but I couldn't send her back out in this weather, and as usual, I had a hard time telling her no. First, I took her coat from her and hung it with the others on the rack.

"Come with me."

"Thank you." She sighed.

I didn't mean to take her to my old bedroom, it just happened to be the first door I opened upstairs. She took a look around, and I wondered what was on her mind. That question unleashed an avalanche of others, most of all: Why had she come here if she didn't think we could be together? I couldn't handle having this much hope again.

"I didn't lie to you. I really hate skiing. Apparently, there isn't much I won't do for a contract."

"It worked out for you, so that's good. And I believe you draw the line somewhere."

Did I make her blush?

"True. I didn't draw it clearly enough. I didn't need to engage in winter sports to get Frasier's signature. It was a cop out. I regret that now, because I would have loved to spend that time with you instead."

How could she still not understand that these words hurt? Because they were just words, leading nowhere. I might be petty, but I wasn't ready to let her down gently, even if it was Christmas Eve.

"I'm not sure what you want me to say."

"You're wearing the necklace."

Self-conscious of the fact, I reached up to touch the expensive piece of jewelry.

"It's beautiful. And it reminds me—never mind. You can have it back if you want to."

Alison shook her head in frustration.

"You don't understand. I didn't come here for the necklace. What kind of person takes a gift back on Christmas? I'm here for you, Cindy."

Part of me had fantasized about a moment like this, before the trip and after...and another part was terrified that I might have imagined it. Maybe she wasn't even here for real, and I was dreaming.

"But you don't have time. You don't want to date anyone."

"It's true, I don't want to get close to anyone. Because my job takes up a lot of time, and...I'm scared as hell of losing them." She held my gaze as she continued. "I always thought I didn't need anyone...until I met the person I needed. There you have it. But I guess you figured that out before I did. You messed with all my best laid plans."

"I'm...sorry?" I wasn't, not at all, even though I was far from being able to appreciate the magnitude of it all. I had worked hard these last few days to try and go along with her truth, that there was no way. Was there?

In the dining room, someone had turned up the music.

"Nancy and I exchanged some texts," Alison said. "I apologized, she apologized, and I said I didn't regret bringing you to meet them. I just wish...it had been real."

Unable to torture her or myself any longer, I walked into her arms, holding on tightly.

"It is real. We'll make time to get to know each other," I promised. "I work miracles, remember? I'll take a look at your schedule, and I'm sure we'll fit in a real date. And you don't have to be scared—"

She interrupted my words with a deep, passionate kiss.

"Are you ready to join us?" The scene Mom walked in on didn't need any explanation. "I'm happy for you," she said, "but please, come before it gets cold."

"I am really sorry to impose—" Alison started, but Mom cut her off.

"First of all, you haven't seen the amount of food my husband buys for the holidays. You might be confronted with a few curious questions."

"I just came from dinner, but I'm okay with questions," Alison said. "I think I have a lot to answer for."

Mom laughed. "Surely you have room for a nightcap?"

"That I can do."

I was going to believe in Christmas miracles from now on, because mine had been delivered right to my door.

Epilogue

NEW YEAR'S EVE

I n the end, both of our wishes had come true. Alison found a girlfriend for Christmas. I got Alison, and I got to spend not only Christmas with her, but ring in the New Year as well.

After a week filled with anticipation, having coffee and dinners, neither of us felt the need to wait any longer.

I'd been dreaming about this moment for so long, it was almost unreal. Using the term fireworks would not be an exaggeration. Through the panoramic windows, we could see the actual fireworks from her bed. We watched them snuggled under the covers, champagne glasses on the nightstand.

"You're still worried about your time management?" I asked, teasing her.

Alison leaned in for another kiss, her fingers tangling into my hair at the back of my neck.

"I think I'll be okay. I just had to adjust my priorities when something—someone—more important came along."

I couldn't help it. I beamed knowing that I was partly responsible for this development.

"Happy New Year, Cindy," she whispered.

"It is already. This has been the best start of a new year ever."

"For me too."

Her cell phone was lighting up with greetings again. *You are missing this awesome party. You could have brought Cindy! Say hello to her?*

"I guess I'll have to tell them I will, and there's nothing at all that I'm missing."

"Sure." I took the cell phone from her and put it next to her glass. "But not now."

I started kissing her again, eager to savor every moment.

Happy endings were for romance novels. This was our beginning, for real, and there was nothing more urgent or important.

About the Author

Barbara Winkes writes sapphic crime drama and Christmas romance. She loves writing characters who get the job done, whether it's stopping a predator or saving cherished traditions—while still making time for love. She lives with her wife in Quebec City.

barbarawinkes.com

Also by Barbara Winkes

Bells Will Be Ringing
Christmas Cupid
Destination Christmas, Next Stop Love
The Christmas Memory